OTIS DOODA

STRANGE BUT TRUE

OTIS DOODA

STRANGE BUT TRUE

by ELLEN POTTER

ILLUSTRATIONS by DAVID HEATLEY

FEIWEL AND FRIENDS ✦ *New York, NY*

SQUARE
FISH

An Imprint of Macmillan
175 Fifth Avenue
New York, NY 10010
mackids.com

OTIS DOODA: STRANGE BUT TRUE.

Library of Congress Cataloging-in-Publication Data Available
ISBN 978-1-250-06272-7 (paperback) / ISBN 978-1-250-01178-7 (ebook)

Originally published in the United States by Feiwel and Friends
First Square Fish Edition: 2015
Book designed by Véronique Lefèvre Sweet and David Heatley
Square Fish logo designed by Filomena Tuosto

10 9 8 7 6 5 4 3 2 1

AR: 4.2 / LEXILE: 630L

For Ian, Clay, and Louisa,

the Silly Squad

TABLE OF CONTENTS

OTIS DOODA

STRANGE BUT TRUE

HARDY-HAR-HAR

Okay, let's just get this over with. My name is Otis Dooda.

Go on. Laugh. I've heard it all before. People call me all sorts of things. When I was in kindergarten, kids called me Otis Doo-Doo. But as I got older, they got more creative. I've been called:

OTIS POOPY-STINKS

OTIS TOILET TWINKIE

OTIS CHEWBACCA CHUNKS

Finished laughing? No? That's very mature of you. Well, get it out of your system.

I'll wait.

Done? Okay, let's move on.

Except for my name, I'm pretty "sort of." I'm sort of skinny and sort of short. I'm sort of good at soccer and sort of bad at math. In other words, I'm sort of average. I lived a sort of average life, too. But then, this summer, my father started a new job, which meant we all had to move to New York City. That's when my life became sort of crazy.

Everything I'm about to tell you is true.

Strange but true.

HOW I KNOW THAT MY BROTHER IS A DOOFUS

When our moving van pulled up in front of Tidwell Towers my mouth popped open. The apartment building we were going to live in was thirty-five stories tall and made of shiny white blocks. It looked exactly like it had been built out of giant white Lego bricks.

WHOA. I said.

My older brother, Gunther, sneered at me. "You think it looks like it's built out of giant white Lego bricks, don't you?"

"No."

"Admit it, Lego Nerd," he said. He placed his foot on mine and started to press down.

"You're wrong," I said.

Gunther squashed my foot even more.

he demanded.

"Because you remind me of a Clydesdale horse, with those big hairy feet of yours," I said.

Gunther's foot pressed down harder and he grinned. His teeth are really tiny. It's like his baby teeth never grew into his teenaged body. Much like his brains.

"Remove your hoof," I told him.

He pressed harder until I almost started to squeal.

Luckily, at that moment our dad said,

I grabbed my backpack, which was stuffed with Lego bricks, comics, and Pokémon cards. I carried my most valuable item in my hand: a Lego lie detector, which I had just finished building the week before. It's made with Legos, a motor, and a wire connected to a tinfoil finger strap. It really works, too. The reason that I know this is that I tried it out on my mother. I hooked her up and asked her if she secretly thought Gunther was a giant doofus. She said, "Of course not," but the lie detector buzzed,

which means she was lying. Then she turned all red in the face and took off the finger strap and said, "Let's not call each other doofuses, shall we?"

Mom examined Gunther and me before we went into the building. She mashed down my hair and she made Gunther put a cover over the cage of his pet rat, Smoochie. She's all excited about moving to the city, but she's worried that people will think we're a bunch of hillbillies. That's because we come from a dinky little town called Hog's Head. Plus, I think we *may* be hillbillies, because Gunther and I whiz off the back porch when the weather is nice.

The apartment building's glass doors slid open as we walked up to them. That was kind of cool, like we were moving into a Price Chopper Supermarket. In the building's lobby was a doorman. He was as burly as a football player. His head was totally bald and he had an earring in one ear. He looked like a nicely dressed pirate. Frankly, he was a little scary. But when my dad told him we were the Doodas he smiled. It was a wide flash of smile. I decided that I might like him.

"Welcome," he said. "My name is Julius. And these"—he held up a pair of shining keys and shook them—"are for apartment 35B."

"You mean we're going to live on

the thirty-fifth floor?"
I cried.

"Yup," Dad said.

"We were keeping that part a surprise," Mom said.

"Sweet!" said Gunther.

I think they were glad to see Gunther excited. When Dad first told us he got a new job in New York City and we were all moving, Gunther wasn't too happy about it. He has this girlfriend back in Hog's Head. Her name is Pandora. She picks at her scalp. Gunther picks at his pimples. They're like Romeo and Juliet, only more disgusting.

As for me, I was happy to be moving away from Hog's Head. A few months ago something really bad happened to me there. I'm not sure if I'm going to tell you about it or not.

We'll just see how things go.

THE CURSE OF POTTED PLANT GUY

At first, Gunther and I helped bring in the boxes from the van. But then we started to moan and groan, so Mom and Dad told us to just stay in the lobby and try not to kill each other.

While we were waiting, the building's glass door slid open and a woman walked into the lobby carrying a bag of groceries. She stopped suddenly, reached into her grocery bag, and pulled out a pack of bubble gum. Then she tossed it in the air and it landed—*plink!*—in a plastic Halloween jack-o'-lantern pail in the corner.

I hadn't noticed the pail before. It sat next to a tall potted plant with long, droopy leaves. I stared at that plant for a minute. There was something strange about it. Then I noticed a pair of eyes peering out from between the leaves, staring back at me. The first thing I thought was that this was some kind of flesh-eating plant, and it was looking at me like I was a four-foot-tall burrito.

But then I told myself, "Otis, flesh-eating plants don't have eyeballs. And that jack-o'-lantern pail is for trick-or-treating. So those eyeballs probably belong to some kid who is sitting in the plant's pot, trying to freak me out."

The glass doors slid open again and a guy walked into the lobby. He had two little poodles with him. Here's the funny thing. One poodle was dyed blue and the other one was dyed pink. They looked like they had fallen into a cotton candy machine. I felt sorry for those dogs, I tell you. But even though they looked all wimpy, they weren't. When they saw the kid in the potted plant, they made a mad lunge for him with their teeth snapping.

"Lola! Noodle! Behave yourselves," the man said as he dug into his pocket. Then he pulled out a quarter and tossed it into the Halloween pail.

Weird.

Halloween was four months away.

And the kid in the potted plant didn't even say thank you. He just kept staring at me. Then I realized he wasn't really staring at *me*. He was actually staring at my Lego lie detector. Suddenly the kid's hand poked out from between the

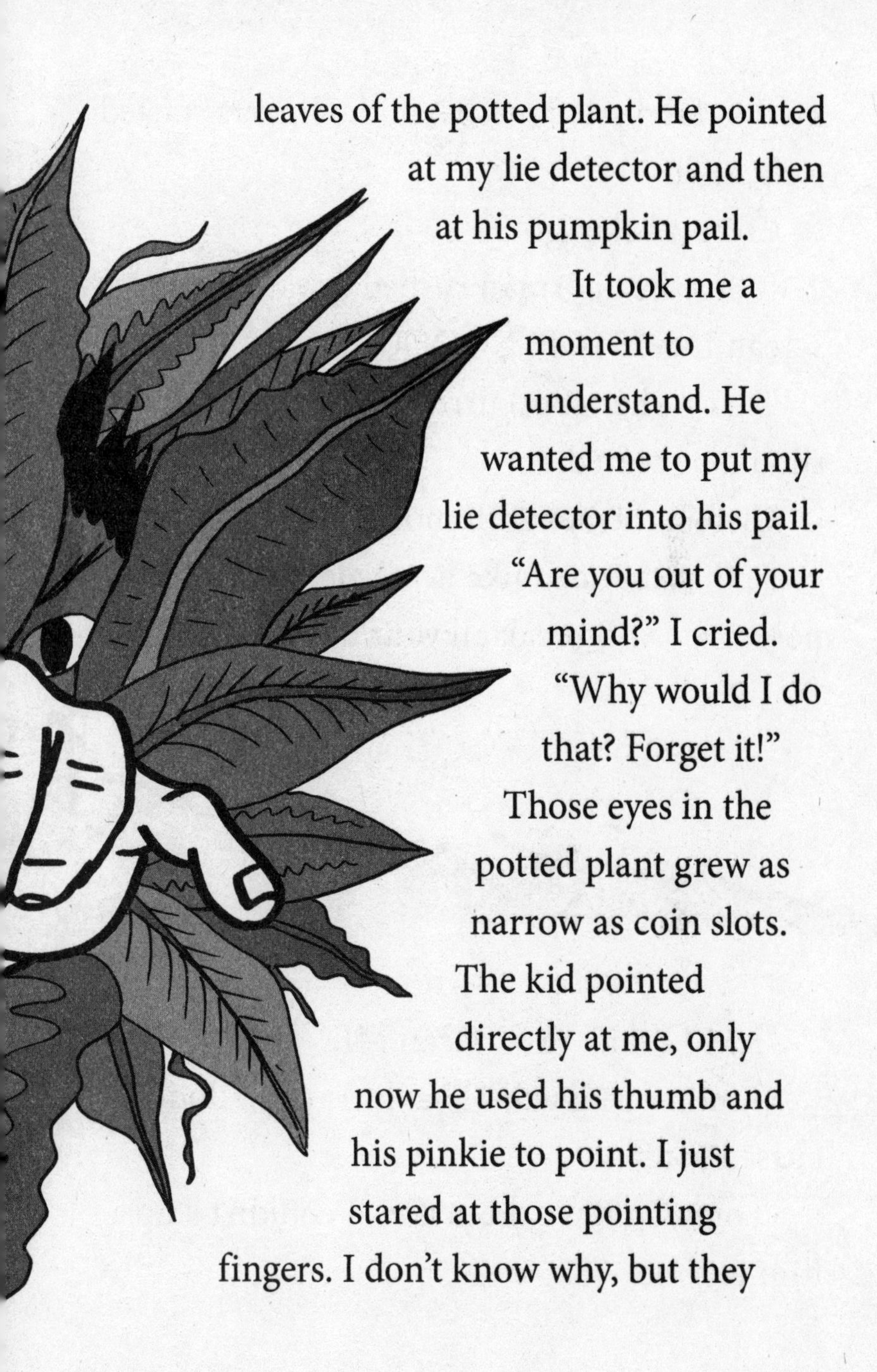

leaves of the potted plant. He pointed at my lie detector and then at his pumpkin pail.

It took me a moment to understand. He wanted me to put my lie detector into his pail.

"Are you out of your mind?" I cried. "Why would I do that? Forget it!"

Those eyes in the potted plant grew as narrow as coin slots. The kid pointed directly at me, only now he used his thumb and his pinkie to point. I just stared at those pointing fingers. I don't know why, but they kind of fascinated me. Then the fingers started to tremble.

Creepy, I thought.

Julius the doorman rushed toward us, screaming, "STOP! NOOOO!"

That's when it occurred to me that maybe I should be scared.

"Before the next full moon," the kid said in a voice that sounded like he needed to blow his nose, "you will break all your bones."

"Me?" I said. "You mean ME?"

Gunther laughed. "That little plant dude just cursed you!"

"Sorry," Julius said to me. "I couldn't stop him in time."

"Just because *he* says I'm going to break all my bones, doesn't mean it's going to happen," I said. Well, to be honest I sort of screeched it. The thing about me is that I freak out pretty easily. Plus, Julius was staring at me in this very tragic way, shaking his bald head.

"That's it, little man," Julius said to me. "Just put it out of your mind."

He gave my shoulder a quick squeeze.

I've seen that shoulder squeeze in movies. It's the shoulder squeeze people give to the guy who

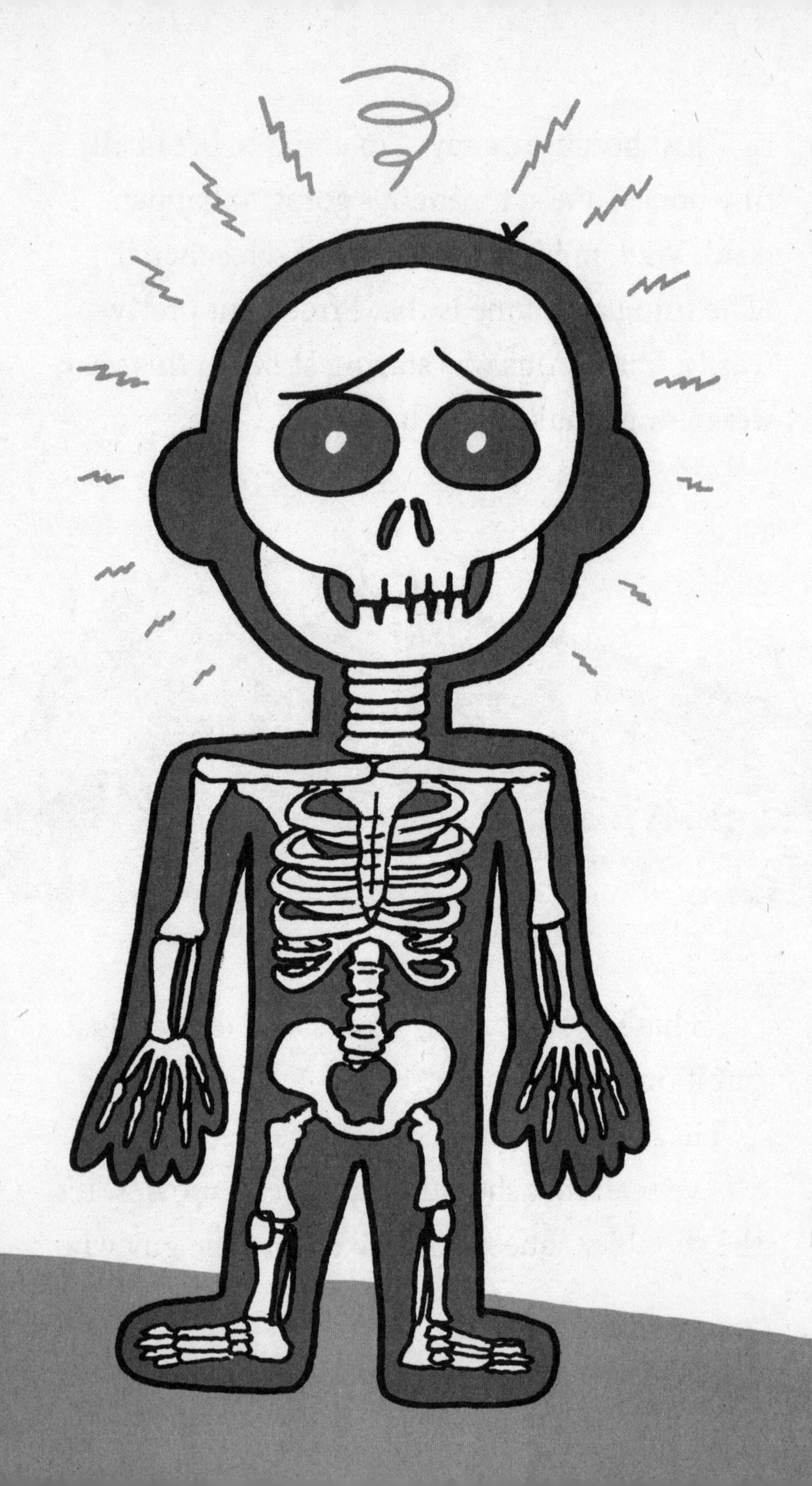

is about to walk into the Cave of Doom to fight the giant spider with the T. rex head and the mucus-dripping fangs. I'm sure you know which shoulder squeeze I mean.

I suddenly began to wonder how many bones were in my body.

"Oh yeee-aah!" Gunther said, stretching his arms wide and nodding happily. "This place is starting to grow on me already."

THE STINK EYE

Now that I'd been cursed, living on the thirty-fifth floor didn't seem like such a good idea after all. And if that wasn't bad enough, guess what else we had? A balcony! My parents kept standing out on it saying, "Otis, come here! You HAVE to see this view!"

I didn't tell them about the curse. They would just say I'm freaking out over nothing.

Gunther loved every minute of it, of course. He kept saying things like, "Wow, if a person fell off that balcony, I bet they'd break every bone in their body. I wonder what bones sound like when they all break at once? *Snappity-snap-snap?* Or maybe one loud *CRRRAAACK!*"

Then he called Pandora and asked her to Google how many days until the next full moon. After a minute, he held up five fingers. And smiled at me.

* * *

After we had unpacked our stuff, my mom said that I had to put the moving boxes in the recycling room. The recycling room was at the other end of the thirty-fifth-floor hallway. It was fun at first. I raced up and down, dragging the smashed cartons. The narrow hallway made everything echo in this clanky way. It sounded like my feet were metal. So I started pretending that I was half human and half robot. I slammed my feet against the hallway floor keeping my legs all stiff like a robot. It made A LOT of noise. But I had to stop when an old lady poked her

head out of an apartment door and gave me the Stink Eye. I get the Stink Eye a lot from grown-ups. If you don't know what that is, it's when someone looks at you with this nasty expression on their face. It's like they just skip over the part where they yell at you and go straight to hating you.

Anyway, I growled at the lady. That's usually what I do when I get the Stink Eye. It makes grown-ups think that there might be something wrong with you. Besides just being annoying, I mean. The lady looked surprised, then quickly ducked back into her apartment and shut the door.

It took all the fun out of being half human, half robot though.

The next time I went out into the hallway with the smashed

boxes, there was a redheaded kid standing by the elevators.

Remember when I told you that everything in this book is true? Here comes a part where you might think I'm lying. But I'm not. This kid was holding a long leash attached to a horse. Not a full-sized horse. It was one of those mini ones, like the size of a big dog.

You couldn't see its head because it was covered with a huge plastic cone. It was the kind of cone they put on dogs' heads so that they won't bite their itchy bits. You could tell it was a horse, not a dog, though, because it had a long horse tail and tiny hooves.

This kid and I stared at each other very curiously.

"What's up with the horse?" I asked him.

"What horse?" he said.

"That one there," I said, pointing to the horse.

I tried not to roll my eyes. I do that a lot, and I know it's rude. But come on. How can you not notice that there's a horse standing next to you?

"He's not a horse," the kid said. "He's a dog."

"Um. No, he's totally a horse," I said.

I looked at this kid more carefully. He seemed normal enough. He had light red hair that was shaggy and he was skinny like me.

the kid said.

"They're very rare. His name is Peaches. Want to walk him with me?"

"Okay. Let me ask my mom."

Even though I still thought Peaches was a horse, I sort of liked this kid. I'm not sure why. Maybe because he had red hair. My favorite Lego Minifigure is this ninja guy with red hair. Only I lost his bottom half so now he has Lego Intergalactic Girl legs.

POO-FUME

I ran back to our apartment and told my mother I was going to walk a French Gerbil Hound with the kid down the hall. She said that she never heard of that kind of dog. I told her they were very rare. She opened the door and looked down the hallway. The kid waved at her. She waved back, but then she frowned at Peaches as if she didn't believe he was a dog either.

"We're just going to Central Park and back," the kid told my mom. "My name is Perry Hooper. I live in apartment 35G, right there." He pointed to the apartment at the other end of the hall.

After a minute, my mom said, "Okay, Otis. Go on. But I want you back here in half an hour."

She gave Peaches another strange look before she closed the door.

While we were waiting for the elevator, I noticed this paper taped to the wall above the elevator button. It said Tidwell Tidbits.

“What’s that?” I asked.

“Oh, it’s this newsletter that Miss Yabby writes. She puts it up on every floor.”

This one said:

TIDWELL TIDBITS

Congratulations to Mrs. Wexler! She lost 130 pounds this summer. If you see her in the elevator, give her a pat on the rump and tell her, "Good work, sweet cheeks!"

Happy 97th Birthday, Mr. Filbert!!! Visit this handsome fellow in apartment 14D and wish him a happy birthday! Remember to keep ringing the bell until he opens the door.

Miss Yabby

I imagined that crusty old guy having to shuffle over to the door a hundred times a day so that someone could wish him a happy birthday.

When the elevator came, Peaches had a hard time getting in because his cone kept getting caught on the edge of the elevator door. We had to guide him in. There was already a lady in the elevator. She gave Peaches the same look my mom did. But she was one of those fancy types of ladies, and after the first look she pretended not to notice him.

Then something really embarrassing happened. Peaches lifted his tail and let out an explosive blast. I'm telling you, I have never smelled anything like it in my life. It was like a massive air bomb made up of cabbage and dirty socks.

"Excuse me," Perry said to the lady, as though he were the one who had done it.

I thought that was pretty big of him to take the blame for something like that.

The lady didn't seem impressed though. She looked angry and you could see she was trying not to breathe through her nose.

Then it happened again. This one sort of hissed out. Reee-aally sloooowly.

Now the woman looked scared. I almost felt sorry for her. The whole elevator suddenly felt twenty degrees warmer because of the power of this thing. I tell you, if someone struck a match, we would have all exploded in a giant fireball of Poo-Fume. That's what my dad calls it. Poo-Fume. Thank heavens the elevator reached the lobby right then. The lady ran out *really* fast. Peaches trotted out, too. He seemed livelier now. I guess all that gas had been weighing him down.

Julius was in the lobby. And guess who else? Yeah, I had almost forgotten about the kid in the potted plant.

"What's wrong?" Perry asked when I stopped short.

I nodded at the plant and said, "He might curse me again."

"Don't worry. Potted Plant Guy only curses people coming into the building, not out of it. And I always keep some extra

Skittles in my pocket, so you can give that to him on the way back in." But then Perry's eyes got all wide. "Wait. You mean he *already* cursed you?"

I nodded. "I'm supposed to break all my bones before the next full moon."

Perry swallowed hard. I actually saw that thingy in his throat bob up and down, which, like Julius's shoulder squeeze, is something else I've seen in the movies. And you know what? It's never a good sign.

BLECHH!

Back in my old town, we had a little park. Hardly anyone ever used it except to go to the bathroom. And there was NO bathroom in the park, if you get my meaning. Little kids whizzed behind the trees and bigger kids

whizzed on the statue of the mayor. And of course dogs whizzed all over the place. But no one ever really played in the park. Probably because it smelled all whizzy.

Central Park was totally different though. There were tons of people there. They were jogging and biking and pushing strollers, and not a single one of them was whizzing. It was sort of refreshing, really.

Still, I would have enjoyed it a lot more if Perry hadn't kept saying things like, "If *I* knew I was going to break all my bones anyway, I'd go hang gliding. From a volcano. While it was erupting."

And . . .

"Think of all the casts you'll have to wear after you break all your bones. You'll look like you're made out of papier-mâché."

"Listen," I said, "I'm *not* breaking all my bones! Curses aren't real."

"Oh yeah? I know a kid who got cursed by Potted Plant Guy last month. The curse was 'You will get attacked by a giant white fly.'

Three days later he was at a Yankees game when a ball came out of nowhere and hit him right in the nose. *Bam!*"

"So? That doesn't prove anything."

"It was a fly ball," Perry said. "A 'giant white fly'? Get it?"

I got it.

There was this *shripp, shripp* sound. Peaches was ripping the grass out of the ground.

"Um, Perry," I said. "Should Peaches be eating grass?"

"To tell you the truth," Perry said, "Peaches isn't a dog. He's a horse."

"Ha! I *knew* he was a horse!" I cried.

"Shh!" Perry warned, glancing around. "The thing is, it's against the law to keep a horse in an apartment, even a miniature horse like Peaches. So we've been telling people that he's a dog. The cone keeps people from looking too closely."

Just in front of us a lady let her beagle off its leash. The dog came running over to Peaches in that goofy, let's-be-doggie-friends sort of way.

Peaches lifted his head from grazing and stared at the beagle. I couldn't get a great view of Peaches' face because of the cone and all, but I was almost certain he was giving the dog the Stink Eye.

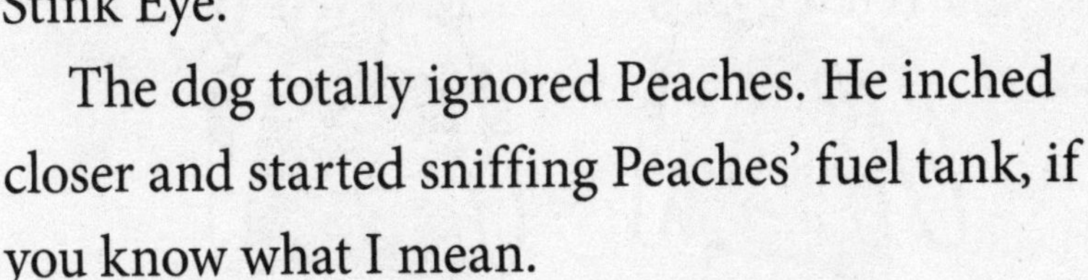

The dog totally ignored Peaches. He inched closer and started sniffing Peaches' fuel tank, if you know what I mean.

"We should shoo him away," I said.

"We really should." Perry nodded.

But we just watched.

Because we are probably not good people.

When Peaches' tail started to lift, Perry and I both stretched out our bottom lips and squinted our eyes. The suspense was awful.

Suddenly, the dog made this bloodcurdling yelp and started shaking his head like crazy. His paws swiped at his nose like he was trying to wipe the stench off.

In a minute, Peaches' fumes hit us, too.

Perry cried, and we both had to pull our shirts over our noses.

"So," I said, my head still in my shirt, "wouldn't it be easier to just have a *dog* as a pet?"

"Peaches isn't a pet. He's working for us. We hired him out for a week," Perry said. He poked his head out of his shirt and took a small sniff. "It's safe."

I poked my head out, too.

"Hired him to do what?" I asked.

"Give pony rides to little kids," Perry answered.

"That seems sort of cruel. To the kids, I mean."

"Well, my dad runs a kids' birthday party business out of a bus. It's called The Big Green Party Machine. Only the business doesn't make much money, so he has to rent out *discount* entertainment. Like Peaches."

At that moment Peaches looked up.

"Hey, he knows his name," I said.

But Perry shook his head grimly. "Wait for it," he said.

In a second, Peaches dropped a pile of *blechh*. Then Perry had to clean it up, and it was all so disgusting that I'm going to totally skip over this whole part and go directly to the next chapter.

WHY I SLEPT IN A BOX

I started off in my bed, but in the middle of the night I heard a click. When I opened my eyes, I saw that my bedroom door was opening really slowly. I stared at that door as it opened wider and wider.

Then I saw it.

The thing was BIG with all these long, skinny things hanging off its head and no legs at all. It took a moment to realize what I was seeing.

Potted Plant Guy!

I made this squeaking sound. Like a guinea pig.

I'm not proud of that either.

Potted Plant Guy was much huger than I thought. And somehow he was making the plant move, and he was moving right toward me!!! In the shadows I could see his eyes peering through the leaves, staring. Large hands stretched out, reaching for me.

I started screaming my head off. In a second my parents ran in. They switched on the light. Now I could see that what I thought was Potted Plant Guy was actually Gunther. He was

wrapped in a blanket and he was wearing this Rasta wig that he won from the Squirt the Duck game at the state fair last summer. I'm telling you, in the dark, the dreadlocks looked exactly like plant leaves. Which Gunther knew, of course.

“What in the world are you doing, Gunther?” my father said in a groggy voice.

“Oh, I’ve been thinking of growing some dreadlocks, Dad,” Gunther lied. “I just wanted to get Otis’ opinion.” He smiled this really cheesy smile.

“At two thirty in the morning!!?” I cried. “Yeah, they’ll believe *that*!”

Guess what? They did.

"You are *not* growing dreadlocks," Mom said.

"Awww, Mom—" Gunther whined, pretending to be all disappointed.

"No discussion," Dad said, taking the wig off Gunther's head. "Back to bed."

"Okay," Gunther said as he trudged out of my room. But before he left, he looked back at me and grinned, showing all his tiny corn-niblet teeth.

I tried to go back to sleep, but I kept seeing suspicious shadows in my room. I had to flick

on the lights about a hundred times to check. Finally, I emptied out a big moving box that was filled with my winter clothes. I poked peepholes into the box and put it over my head. I figured if someone did come into my room, they wouldn't know I was there. It was nice and dark in the box. But I couldn't lie down. So I spent practically the whole night looking out those peepholes.

DOODLE DUDE

I am starting to worry about my mother. I think she may be losing her mind. If you see a crazy lady wandering around New York City, muttering,

please return her to the following address: 566 Amsterdam Avenue, apartment 35B.

Julius, the doorman, will know what to do with her.

My mom started acting weird right after she saw a sign in the building's laundry room. It said, "Kid Zone. Fun classes. Zumba, gymnastics, tap dance, yoga, and more!"

"Ooo, kids' yoga!" she said. Then she looked at me with those crazy eyes.

"Don't even think what you're thinking, lady," I warned her.

"But you might like yoga," she said.

"I don't even like the *word* yoga," I told her.

"Otis, now that we're in New York, I want you to experience new things. And anyway, you know *the rule.*"

I growled.

My mother ignored it, but the lady folding clothes on the table nearby gave me a funny look.

I growled at her, too, and she looked away.

My parents' rule is that you have to try something three times before you can decide you hate it. Here are a few things that I have discovered (the hard way) that I hate:

1. SOY WIENERS

2. SHARING A TENT WITH GUNTHER

3. HAVING MY NOSE SUCTIONED OUT

(I USED TO HATE BLOWING MY NOSE WHEN I WAS SICK, UNTIL MOM STUCK THAT SUCTION THING UP MY NOSTRILS A FEW TIMES. NOW I HAVE NO PROBLEM BLOWING MY NOSE, THANK YOU VERY MUCH.)

The next morning, Mom said we were going to Kid Zone to sign up for a yoga class.

"What about Gunther?" I whined. "He should have to go to yoga, too."

"I don't think Gunther is very bendy," my mother whispered to me as we passed his bedroom.

Gunther was sitting on his bed with Smoochie the rat laying on top of his head. He was talking on his cell phone to Pandora while picking a pimple on the side of his neck. Pandora was probably picking at her scalp. Very romantic.

"Well, I'm not bendy either," I told my mother.

My mother just ignored me. We all know that I am *very* bendy. My body looks like it's made out of Twizzlers.

We took the subway down to Kid Zone. While we waited on the platform this shady-

looking guy walked right up to us. He looked all around, like he was about to do something he shouldn't. Then out of the corner of his mouth he muttered, "Doodle dude."

"Excuse me?" my mother said.

"Doodle dude," he said again.

Then he opened up one hand and showed us what was in it. Three Cheez Doodles that were dressed up like little men. They had tiny sunglasses and little outfits and everything.

"Cool!" I said.

"Three dollars each," the guy said to my mom.

"No, thank you," she said.

"But, Mom," I whined. "It's a Doodle Dude! It's like a Lego Minifigure that you can eat."

Mom wouldn't go for it.

One thing I'm looking forward to when I am a grown-up is having enough cash to buy a Doodle Dude if I feel like it.

SUBWAY ZOMBIES

So I was enjoying the whole subway thing right up until the moment I sat down in the subway car and it started to move. That's when I noticed something creepy. There were a whole bunch of people who looked like zombies. They stared out of the subway windows with no expression, and their eyeballs jiggled back and forth. I mean it! It was the scariest thing I have ever seen.

My mom jabbed me in the side. "Stop staring at people," she said.

"But their eyes are all jiggly."

"It's just because they're looking at things out the window, and everything is passing by very quickly," my mom said. "It makes their eyes go back and forth like that."

I don't buy it.

I think there may be some sort of zombie city under New York. Maybe they live in the subway tunnels and eat live rats. And when they're sick of gnawing on rat bones, they ride the trains to look for fresh meat. Like kids.

Suddenly, one of the zombie guys looked right at me.

Especially Twizzler-shaped kids.

The Kid Zone was this dumpy old building a few blocks away from the subway station. It looked like someone had scooped out its insides like a Halloween pumpkin. There was nothing in it except a huge, open space filled with kids

and one lady with a lot of armpit hair. They were all just standing there with their arms out to the side and one leg lifted up.

"You are all storks," the lady said. "Your wings are spread. You are getting ready to fly."

One "stork" toppled over and fell on his face.

After that, the lady had the kids put their hands on the floor and their rear ends in the air.

Then they all began to bark.

I'm not even kidding.

The woman was barking, too.

I started laughing. Mom shushed me, but I just couldn't help it. Finally the lady stopped barking and looked at us.

"You are both welcome to join us in Downward Dog," she said.

"Oh . . . mmm . . . no, thank you," my mother said in this really high, nervous voice. Then she hurried me right out of that place.

What a relief, right? Close call, right? Yeah, well, you don't know my mom. Have you ever tried to pull a bone out of a pit bull's mouth?

Well, my mom was the pit bull, and putting me into some crazy class was her bone.

And speaking of bones, when we got back on the subway to go home, there was this lady subway zombie sitting across from us. She caught me staring at her jiggly eyes. Then she stopped looking out the window and stared at my ankles, which are pretty bony.

I bet they are better to gnaw on than rat bones, I thought.

That's when I started to wonder if Potted Plant Guy's curse was about to come true. Maybe the subway zombies were going to grab me and take me back to their underground tunnel and chomp my bones to bits.

I tucked my legs under my rear end to hide my ankles from her. But my foot kept accidentally pushing at the guy sitting next to me. Finally he turned to me and said, "The next time you dig your foot into me, buddy, I'm going to twist you into a pretzel."

Zombies might like pretzels even more than Twizzlers.

I put my feet back down on the ground again and tried not to look so tasty.

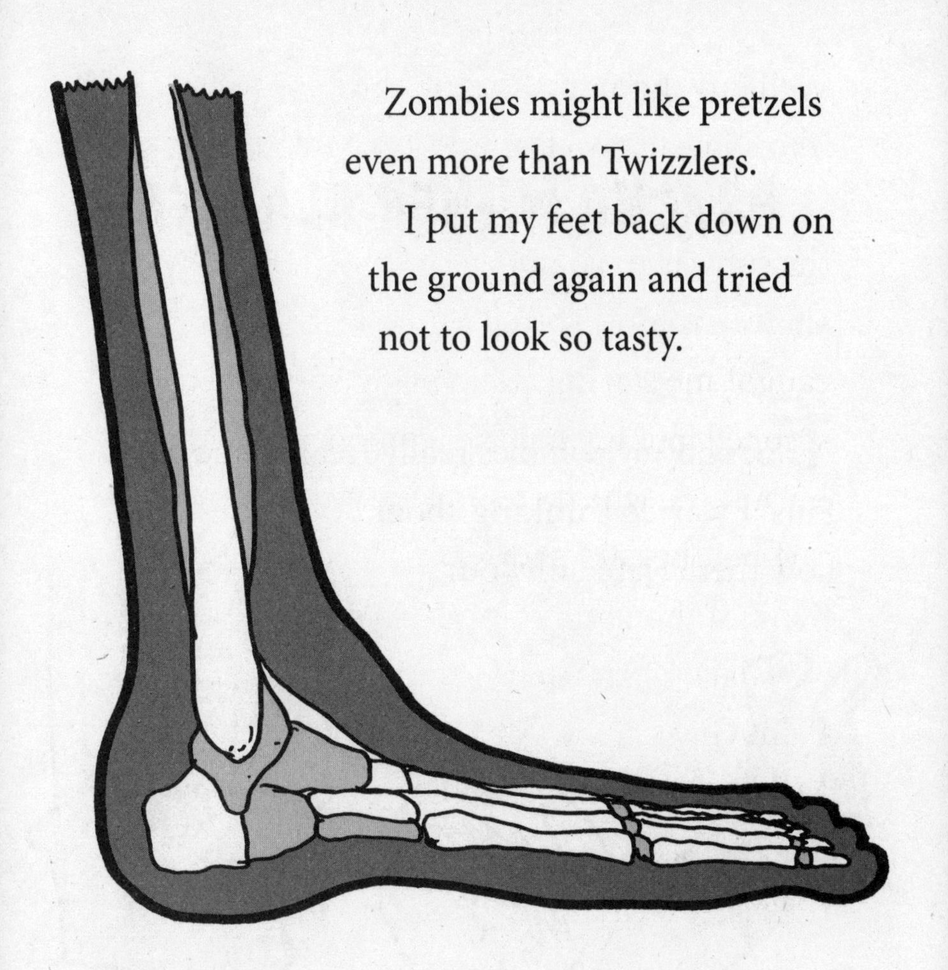

PSYCHO WIENER BLASTER

The subway zombies really freaked me out. Plus, I started thinking about how there were only four

more days until the next full moon, and then I got even more freaked out. So when I came home I started working on my Lego inventions. That always calms me down. I think it's the way everything fits together so perfectly. I wish my life was more like that.

I have this huge cabinet where I keep my Lego bricks, sorted out by size, shape, and color. I once counted them all. I have 1,673 Lego bricks.

The reason I have so many of them is because of this little hair that grows out of my mom's chin. She's had it for as long as I can remember. It's all black except for a white tip. It looks like a magic wand. I call it The Biggle. It embarrasses the heck out of her. She used to pluck it, but it kept coming back so now she just leaves it alone. But the thing is, that Biggle was just so disturbing. I used to try to grab it and yank it out of her chin. It was really hard to do, because if I wasn't fast

enough, Mom would smack my hand away before I could even get a grip on that thing. One time, when she told me to cut it out, I said, "It's good for hand-eye coordination. Like video games. But since you won't let me get any video games, I guess I'll just have to practice my skills on The Biggle."

Mom says playing video games is like sticking your brain in a blender and pressing Liquefy.

This time I thought Mom was going to cave. But the next day she handed me a Lego *Star Wars* set. She said Legos were good for

coordination, too. I wasn't too happy about that at first. But it wasn't long before I was totally hooked.

Still, every so often I'll make a grab for The Biggle. Just for old times' sake.

Now I plunged my hand into the drawer of Lego gears and pulleys and motors. Right away I had an idea. Maybe I couldn't avoid curses and subway zombies, but at least I could have some peace of mind in my own bedroom. So I built the Psycho Wiener Blaster. It took me a couple of hours until I got it just right. Now I just needed the wieners.

My dad was sitting on the living room couch, watching TV and eating a bag of Fritos.

He was in his undershirt because our air conditioner had busted during the move. I don't like to see too much of his man skin, if I can help it. It's sort of splotchy and there are these sad little lumps where I believe his muscles used to be. Mom was busy tinkering with the air conditioner, so I hurried past into the kitchen and poked through the fridge until I found what I needed. A pack of soy wieners. Mom buys them for us because she says we eat too much garbage. Which is funny because soy wieners taste like *actual* garbage. I was just about to shove the pack under my shirt when Mom walked into the kitchen and asked what I was doing with those soy wieners.

"Making lunch," I said.

"I thought you hated soy wieners," she said.

"Where did you get that idea?" I said, trying to look shocked.

"From your face, every time you eat them," my mom said.

"I happen to love soy wieners," I told her. And to prove it I stuck one of them in the toaster oven.

"Yeah, well, I better not find that wiener stuffed behind the couch cushions like last time," Mom said before she left.

Quickly, I shoved the rest of the pack under my shirt and went back to my room. I found some spiky rubber cannonball pieces that I got from my Lego castle set and stuck them into the ends of the soy wieners. Soy wieners may taste like dog food, but those suckers can really hold a Lego piece! They looked pretty dangerous by the time I was finished with them.

Finally, I rigged the Psycho Wiener Blaster to my bedroom door and aimed the launcher. If anyone tried to sneak into my room at night, well . . . this is what would happen (don't look if you are the sensitive type):

Just as I got it all set up and was ready to test it out, there was a knock on my door.

Now I'm not going to sugar-coat things for you. There was a good chance that it was Mom.

There was a *slight* chance that it was Gunther, and that would have been thirty-four flavors of awesome! But Gunther didn't usually knock. Unless it was on my skull.

Anyway, I figured if it *was* Mom, and *if* the Psycho Wiener Blaster worked, I could sell it to the United States Army to help pay for her hospital bills.

BORIS

"Come in!" I said.

My eyes got wide and I held my breath.

The door opened.

Shpoof! The first soy wiener shot out of the launcher. Perry ducked and it went right over his head. *Shpoof*! Out shot the second wiener. *Shpoof, shpoof, shpoof!* The third, the fourth, the fifth! It was a beautiful thing! And I'll tell you what else . . . that Perry has great reflexes! He ducked and jumped and popped his hips to one side, then the other. Not a single soy wiener hit him. Honestly, he was like some kind of secret-agent guy.

When the wieners were all fired, Perry strolled into the room.

he said.

The way he acted, you'd think someone fired wieners at him every day of the week.

Right behind him was this other kid. He was really tall with lots of frizzy hair and he was

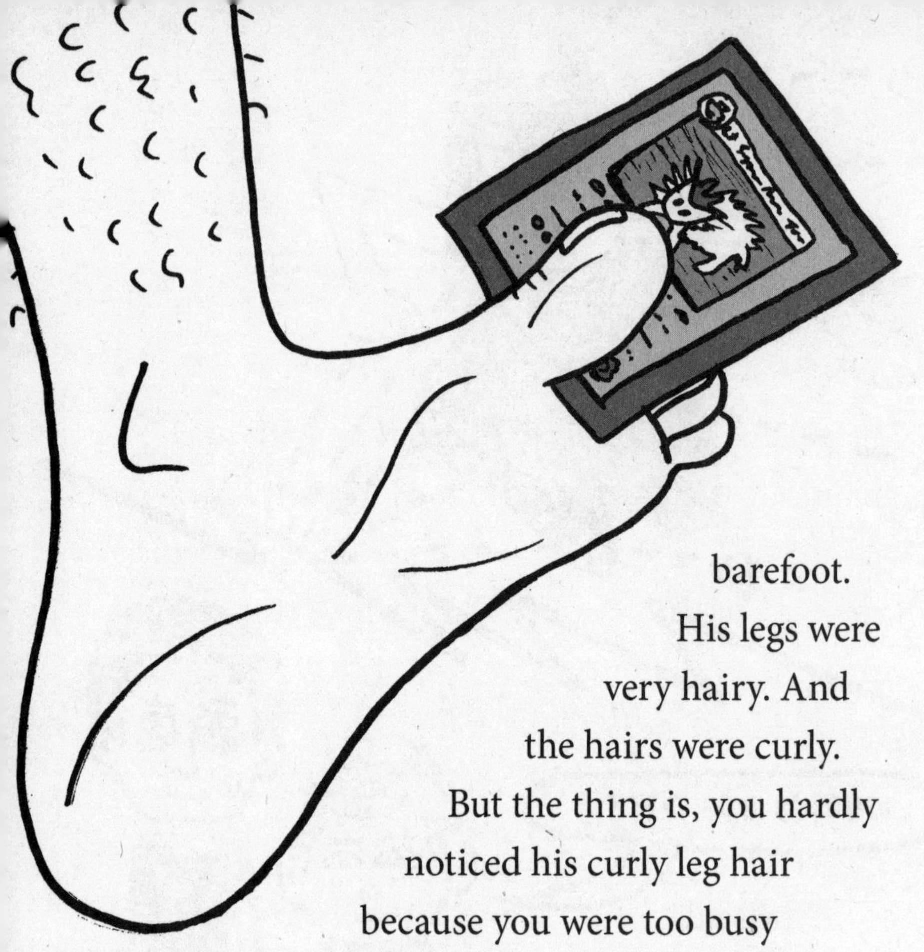

barefoot.

His legs were very hairy. And the hairs were curly.

But the thing is, you hardly noticed his curly leg hair because you were too busy staring at his face. He had purplish black bruises under each eye.

“That’s Boris,” Perry said. “He lives on four.”

I nodded hello, but Boris was staring down at a Pokémon card on the floor.

“This yours?” he said. He picked up my card between his toes.

"That's disgusting!" I said.

"What?" He looked all insulted. Like I should be thrilled that he smeared his toe jam on my stuff.

He dropped the card back on the floor. Then he picked up my Lego lie detector—with his hands at least—and he plopped himself down on my bed. Those curly leg hairs were all over my blanket and everything. Then he started messing around with my lie detector.

"Careful with that!" I told him.

No wonder someone gave him two black eyes.

I would have grabbed the lie detector out of his hands, but he was a pretty big guy. You never know with big guys. Either they're really tough or they are total pushovers.

"What is this thing?" he asked.

"It's a lie detector, okay?"

"Did you make this thing?" He was turning it around and around in his ape hands.

"Yeah," I said.

"Wow. You must be some sort of Frankenstein."

"Frankenstein?"

"You know," Boris said. "That smart guy with the crazy white hair."

"Einstein."

"Nah, that's not his name," Boris said.

"Yes it is."

This guy was really annoying.

"So, Otis," Perry said, "me and Boris and the kid next door are going swimming. You coming?"

"Sure," I said.

Anything to get that freak out of my room.

And anyhow, I wanted to work on my dives. I was just starting to get pretty good at them this summer.

"I'll get my bathing suit," I said, and started for my dresser.

"You don't need a bathing suit for this pool," Perry said as he and Boris headed out the door.

Looking back, that should have been a tip-off.

THE FLUFFINATOR

The pool was right outside my apartment, in the middle of the thirty-fifth-floor hallway.

And it wasn't so much a pool as a big tub filled with Marshmallow Fluff.

And the diving board wasn't so much a diving board as a cannon.

"Just in time, boys!" said Perry's dad, Mr. Hooper. His hair was as red as Perry's, only there was less of it. "Cat was just about to dive in!"

I looked around for the cat. All I saw was a giant marshmallow at the far end of the hall. The marshmallow was wearing red glasses and a white helmet and was jammed inside a big cannon.

Suddenly Mr. Hooper pulled a lever in the back of the cannon.

BOMBS AWAY, SUCKERS!

the marshmallow yelled as it was launched out of the cannon and flew through the air. It didn't make it to the Fluff Pool though. Instead, it landed on its stomach and shot across the hallway floor like a hockey puck.

"Oooo, *so* close, Cat," Mr. Hooper said to the marshmallow. "Let me just tinker with the cannon."

The marshmallow stood up and pulled off its white helmet. There was a girl-face underneath.

"Next victim," Cat said, holding out her helmet to me.

"Perry can go next," I said.

I gave him this cheesy smile. I'm about as brave as a jellyfish, if you want to know the truth.

Perry stuck the helmet on his head, and Cat took off the marshmallow outfit and handed it to him. It turned out that the marshmallow suit was all padding. Without it, Cat was about the size of a cat. I think she may even be skinnier than me.

"So." She eyeballed me. "You the kid who's going to break all his bones?"

"I am *not* breaking all my bones," I said.

She looked disappointed. "Perry said Potted Plant Guy cursed you."

"He did," I admitted.

Cat nodded. "Oh, you'll be breaking those bones, Princess."

Perry was all suited up in his marshmallow gear. His dad helped him get into the cannon.

"Ready?" Mr. Hooper said.

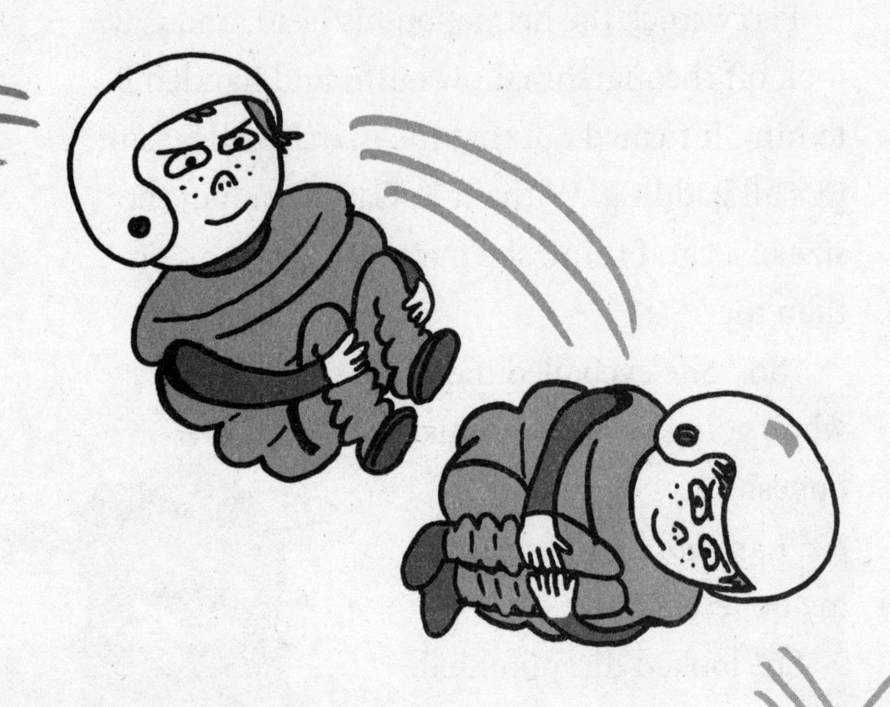

Perry gave him the thumbs-up. Mr. Hooper pulled the lever and *whooooosh!* Perry flew through the air. You wouldn't believe it, but he actually did a somersault mid-flight.

"Whoa!" I said. "It's like he *is* the redheaded ninja Minifigure!"

He didn't make it into the Fluff Pool though. He flew right over it and landed on his belly, like Cat.

He got up, took off his helmet, and held it out to me. I tried to pawn it off on Boris, but he said he was too big to fit in the marshmallow suit.

"Don't worry," Perry said, patting me on the back. "Dad usually gets it right by the third try."

"Hey," said Cat excitedly while I was putting on the marshmallow suit, "maybe this is when he'll break all his bones."

"Not with all this padding," Boris said, and he punched me in the arm. I didn't feel anything, which was reassuring.

"Yeah, well, that helmet felt pretty flimsy," Cat said. "Doesn't your dad usually get his stuff from the bargain catalogs?"

"Not this one!" Perry said proudly. "Some guy sold it to him from the back of a truck."

I groaned.

"And anyway," Perry said, "if the helmet busts, then he'll only break his head. And he's probably got about five hundred more bones to break if he's going to break *all* of them."

"Two hundred and five. I've got two hundred and five more bones to break," I muttered.

As far as I could see, I had three options:

1. LAND IN THE FLUFF POOL AND TURN MYSELF INTO A HUMAN PEEP.

2. LAND ON THE GROUND AND POSSIBLY CRACK MY SKULL.

3. TELL THEM THAT I JUST REMEMBERED I HAD TO CLEAN OUT SMOOCHIE'S CAGE AND RUN AWAY.

I was just about to choose Option 3 when Gunther came out into the hallway with Smoochie's cage and a poop scoop.

He took one look at me in my marshmallow suit and then at the cannon. He put the cage and poop scoop down and crossed his arms over his chest.

he said.

I stepped into the cannon. I gave Mr. Hooper the thumbs-up. The last thing I remember thinking as I flew through the air was, "This must be how a soy wiener feels . . . GAAAAAA!"

OLD LADY BRAINS

Fluff is not as fluffy as you'd think. It's a little bit like diving into Elmer's Glue.

When I stood up, my eyelashes were stuck together and I had Fluff up my nose.

I pulled myself out of the vat, which wasn't easy. You can't imagine how heavy a padded suit covered with Fluff can be! Perry, Cat, Boris, and Mr. Hooper were all clapping and cheering though. Even Gunther looked impressed. I was starting to think that it was almost worth it.

Just then the door of apartment 35E opened. That woman who gave me the Stink Eye popped her head out and shouted, "What's going on here?! What's all this noise?"

When she caught sight of me, she stopped shouting. Her eyes got wide. I guess I looked pretty scary, all huge and puffy and dripping with white goo. So I did the only thing that I could in that situation. I stuck my arms straight out and I started walking toward her, saying, "Me must gobble up old lady. Me love old lady brains. They so dry and crackly." Then I smacked my marshmallow lips together.

Well, she looked like she was about to faint. I would have felt bad if she did. But I guess she had what you would call "a strong will to survive," because all of a sudden she reached for something just inside her apartment. Then she came running at me like a lunatic with this long wooden stick. I think it must have been stuck in a plant to prop it up, because there were still leaves wrapped around it. I turned around to run away, but she jabbed the thing right into the back of my marshmallow suit. Thank goodness

for the padding! I didn't actually feel a thing, but that stick was wedged in there pretty tight.

"What's that smell?" Cat said suddenly.

I couldn't really smell anything, on account of all the Fluff up my nose. Still, I looked around to see if Peaches was somewhere nearby.

"Smells like something's burning," Perry said, wrinkling up his nose.

Just then my mother came flying out of our apartment, holding something that was trailing black smoke. My dad was right behind her, in his undershirt.

"Someone call the fire department!" my mother shrieked.

There was all this black smoke pouring out of our apartment, and the smoke alarm was beeping like crazy.

While Mr. Hooper ran into his apartment to make the call, my mother looked at me in my giant marshmallow suit.

"Hi, Mom." I smiled at her.

"You . . . left . . . the . . . soy . . . hot dog . . . in . . . the . . . toaster . . . oven," she said in a furious voice.

Then she lifted up the fork with the black, smoking wiener speared on one end.

Oops.

S'MORES, ANYONE?

One good thing to know about New York City is that firefighters come really fast. They were rushing onto the thirty-fifth floor in no time flat. At first, they frowned at me in my marshmallow suit and at the cannon and the tub of Fluff. I think they suspected we were playing some sort of joke on them. But then they saw the smoke coming out of our apartment.

They told us to take the stairs all the way down to the lobby, because you're not supposed to use the elevator in a fire. I asked them if I could rinse off and change into some fresh clothes first. That really seemed to annoy them. They sent one of the firefighters to "escort" us down the stairs.

Walking down thirty-five flights of stairs is no picnic in the best of situations. But try doing it while dressed as a giant marshmallow in 90-degree heat. You can't even imagine how heavy and hot that suit felt with all the Fluff on it. Plus I still had that stick wedged into the back of it. I tried to pull the suit off but it was all soggy and stuck to me. And every time I stopped on the stairs to tug at it, the firefighter/prison guard would say, "Keep moving,

Buster." I think he was mad at me because the stick in my suit kept poking him in the stomach.

Gunther thought it was all pretty hysterical and he was laughing his head off until Cat turned to him and said,

That shut him up pretty fast.

I wondered if Cat liked Legos. If she did, she might be the perfect female.

When we finally reached the lobby, Julius the doorman just stared at us, like he was watching a parade. It really *was* like a parade, too, because my mother kept holding that burnt-up soy wiener on the fork, like she was carrying a flag.

A shriveled, black flag that said, “My son is a bonehead.”

Finally Julius said to Mr. Hooper, “Trying out a new game for The Big Green Party Machine?”

“Yes, Julius,” Mr. Hooper muttered. He sounded like a kid who had been caught doing something he shouldn’t.

“Most people put Fluff on sandwiches, Mr. Hooper, not on people,” Julius said as he looked at the Fluff tracks on his clean lobby floor.

“Yes, Julius,” Mr. Hooper said, his head drooping.

So we had to wait in the lobby while about a million people walked past us and stared. The whole time Potted Plant Guy laughed at me behind the leaves. He laughed like this: "Heh, heh, heh." Really. Who laughs like that? Apart from mad scientists in cartoons.

Finally, I got totally annoyed and I walked right up to him and yelled, "At least I don't have to be watered every day."

"Leave that kid alone, Otis," my dad said and he grabbed the stick in my back and yanked me away from him, while Mom stuck the burnt wiener in my face and said, "Don't you think you've embarrassed your family enough in front of our new neighbors?"

"Yes," I said. "Yes, I believe that I have."

Except that was what is called a "rhetorical question," which means you're not really supposed to answer it unless you want the Stink Eye.

WELL, BUTTER MY BUNS!

As it turned out, I wasn't totally done embarrassing my parents. The next morning, about a minute after Dad left the apartment to go to work we heard him out in the hallway shouting,

That wasn't *really* what he was shouting. I can't say what he was shouting. They were bad words.

We all ran out into the hallway, and then my mother started saying, "Beans and rice, *beans and rice!*"

Because right above the elevator button was one of those Tidwell Tidbits, and the headline was

TIDWELL TIDBITS

Hillbilly Bar-B-Que on the 35th Floor Causes 2-Alarm Fire.

When you see the Doodas in the elevator, make them feel at home and give them a big "Well, butter my buns!" (That's "hello" in hillbilly.)

Mr. and Mrs. Dooda in Apartment 35B attempt to turn their son into a human s'more.

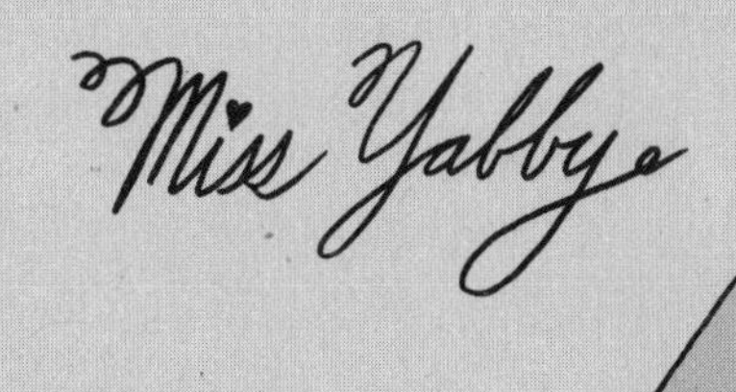

Then the elevator door opened. There were three people inside, and when they saw us, their eyes opened wide.

they all shouted at us.

"Good morning," Dad mumbled as he walked in the elevator.

Later that day, the door bell rang. When Mom opened the door there was a guy dressed all in black with a black ski mask standing there. She let out a scream. Then Perry took off his ski mask.

"You shouldn't open your door without asking who's there first, Mrs. Dooda," Perry said.

"Thanks for the tip," my mother grumbled.

"Anytime, Mrs. D," Perry said, walking into the apartment.

I was sitting on the couch, watching TV. Perry stood in front of me and folded his arms, looking very serious.

"Why are you dressed like a ninja?" I asked him.

"Because something big is going down," Perry said in a whispery voice.

Perry said out of the corner of his mouth.

"What duck?"

"It's spy speak, Otis," Perry said.

"Well, speak in people speak," I said.

Perry sighed. "Just wear something scary and meet me in 35F at thirteen hundred hours."

"What?"

Perry sighed again. "Meet me in Cat's apartment in ten minutes. Sheesh."

Clearly, I was a disappointment as a spy.

Before he left, he peeked into the kitchen.

"Well, butter my buns!" he said to my mother.

Mom looked like she might cry.

ALIEN BRAINS

The scariest thing I could find was last year's Halloween costume of an alien. It was this black jumpsuit with a silver belt and it came with a green rubber mask. The mask was pretty scary, really, because the head was HUGE and the alien's big brains were sitting up there, in plain sight, flopping all over the place.

Mom had gone shopping and Gunther was supposed to watch me. Which meant that he was sitting in his room, talking to Pandora, and picking his face. He didn't notice at all when I left.

I knocked on apartment 35F. Three miniature Cats opened the door. They looked exactly like her, minus the glasses. One was a boy, one was a girl, and it's anybody's guess what the third kid was. They looked up at me in my alien costume.

Then all three turned and walked down the hall, with their matching shiny black heads.

I followed them into a bedroom with three tiny beds, but no Cat.

The miniature girl-Cat pointed up. There was this big wooden box that was attached to the ceiling by chains. It was half the size of the room and it had all these holes cut out of it. It was just hanging there. I thought the mini Cats must be playing a joke on me. But then a face with red glasses appeared in one of the box's holes.

"What took you so long, Otis?" Cat said.

I don't know what was weirder: that she was sitting in a box suspended in the air or that she knew it was me in the alien costume.

"Get your carcass up here," Cat said. She tossed a rope ladder out of the hole.

Rope ladders are not as much fun as you might think, by the way. Especially when three Oompa

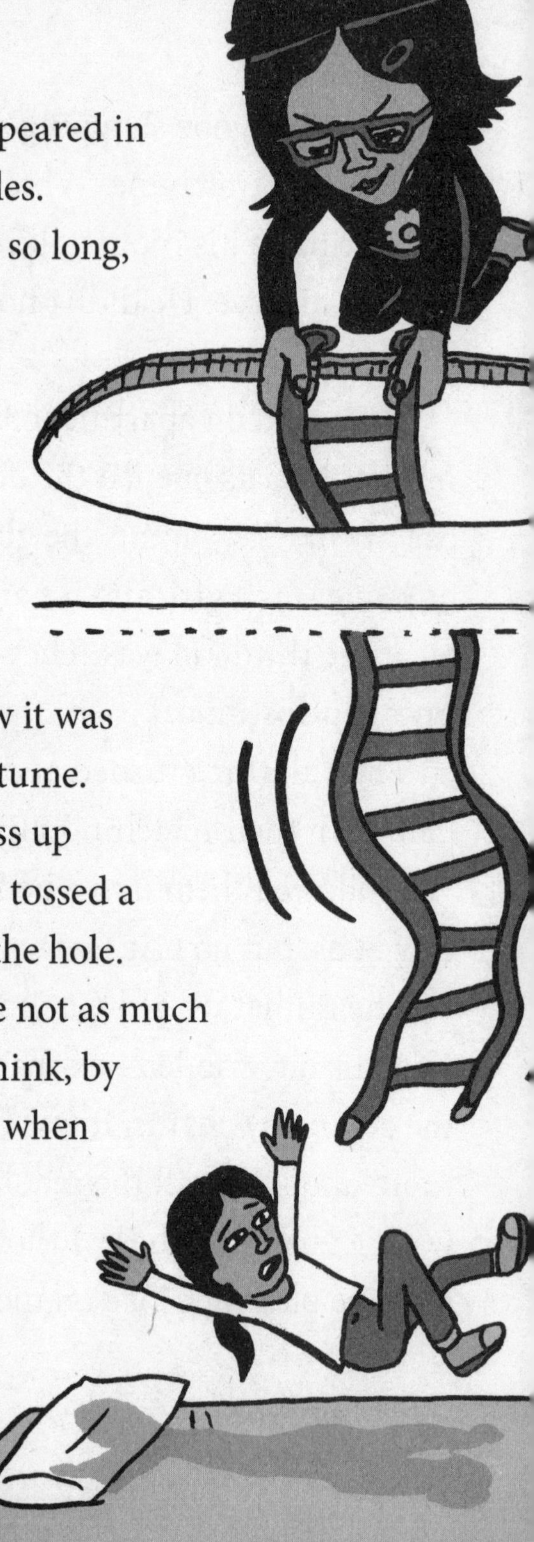

Loompas are trying to scramble up the rope behind you.

"Linus, Lucy, Hobbes! Down!" Cat yelled at them. As soon as I scrambled into the box, Cat shook the rope ladder so hard that all three kids flew off in different directions. Then Cat pulled the rope ladder up into the box again.

"Linus, Lucy, and Hobbes?" I said.

"My mom's Vietnamese. She learned English by reading comics," Cat said.

"What about Cat?" I asked.

"My middle name is Girl."

The box was all carpeted inside and looked just like a cat room. I mean, it was *Cat's room*, but it was also a cat room, like the kind you would buy at a pet store. I think they call it a cat condo. Cat's room was a lot bigger of course. There was a little carpeted platform with a pillow on it that I guess

was her bed. And there was a drum set in one corner and a bow and arrow hung on one of the walls. It looked real, too.

We all sat on the floor in the middle of the box. It was kind of squishy,

especially since there were four of us up there—Perry, Boris, Cat, and me. All of them were dressed as ninjas.

"What's with the alien costume?" Cat asked.

"Perry told me to wear something scary," I told them.

Boris reached over and squeezed my rubber brains.

"Guess what?" he said. "Alien brains aren't on the outside of their heads."

"How do you know?" I asked.

"Well, think about it. Their hats would get all slimy." He looked me up and down. "I like those funky skeleton tentacles, though."

"Those are my arms and legs," I told him. "You know, Boris, it's no wonder someone punched you in the face."

It wasn't a nice thing to say, I'll admit. But I'm kind of sensitive about my skinniness.

Everyone got real quiet then. Boris looked like he was ready to cry.

"No one punched Boris in the face," Cat said.

"He was cursed by Potted Plant Guy," Perry said. "He was the one that got hit in the face by the fly ball."

I looked at Boris. His two black eyes made him look like a depressed gangster.

"Sorry, Boris," I said.

"Apology accepted, Skindiana Bones," he replied.

It's really hard to like that kid.

"*Any*way"—I turned to Perry and Cat—"what are we here for?"

"Okay, Otis, here's the plan." Perry leaned in and rubbed his hands together. "We're going to put The Kibosh on Potted Plant Guy."

"What's a kibosh?" I asked.

"It means we're going to make

sure that he will no longer be a threat to mankind," said Perry.

"And how are we going to do that?" I asked.

Perry looked at Cat. Cat looked at Boris. And Boris looked at me.

"You're the one with all the brains, Galaxar," Boris said, flicking my rubber brains. "You tell *us*."

THE KIBOSH

"We'll make a list," I said.

I had no idea why. It just sounded like a good idea.

Cat leaned out of the hole in the box and called,

She threw down the rope ladder. In less than a minute, one of the mini Cats was scrambling up.

"Is Hobbes a boy or a girl?" I whispered to Perry.

Perry shrugged.

Cat took the pen and paper out of Hobbes's hands. Then she shook the ladder until Hobbes flew off and landed on one of the beds.

"Okay," I said, taking off the alien mask. It was getting too hot in there. "We'll list everything we know about Potted Plant Guy."

Here's what that list looked like:

"Nice work!" I said. I spoke very loudly. I find that makes you sound like you know what you're doing.

Perry, Cat, and Boris didn't look too impressed.

"Why don't we list everything we *don't* know about Potted Plant Guy," Perry suggested.

"Excellent suggestion, my good man!" I said this with an English accent. I don't know why.

This was the list we came up with:

That didn't seem too helpful either. But then I realized something.

"Julius must know who he is," I said. "He must see him climbing in and out of the potted plant every day."

Perry shook his head. "I already asked Julius. He told me it would be better for my health and welfare if I didn't go poking my nose into Potted Plant Guy's business."

I frowned. This was not looking good. We'd never figure out The Kibosh at this rate.

"Okay, let me think."

"Maybe you should put the rubber brains back on your head," Cat said.

She was just being snotty, of course. But I put the mask back on anyway. And you know what? I think it helped. Because suddenly I had a plan.

Poodles of Mass Destruction

The second Perry and I rang the doorbell to apartment 14B, there was the sound of barking dogs. The door opened and a blue poodle barked at my leg while a pink poodle jumped on me and made little snapping sounds with its teeth.

"Lola! Noodle! Down!" the man at the door said.

I guess the pink dog thought that "Down" meant "Stop, pee, step in it, then jump on the strangers again."

"Bad doggies!" the man said.

"But they're bad in a *cute* way, Mr. Felder," Perry said.

It was a total lie, but the guy fell for it.

"Aren't they?" Mr. Felder sighed, smiling. "Now what can I do for you boys?"

Man, Perry was good! I let him do the talking while I fought off the cotton-candy-colored T. rexes.

"We're trying to earn money for our Cub Scout uniforms this fall," Perry said (my idea), "and would like to walk your dogs. We'd charge fifty cents a walk."

Of course, that was totally not worth it. But, if our plan went well, we'd only be walking those two maniacs once. Below is a quick sketch I drew of our Master Plan.

In the lobby we will accidentally lose control of the dogs and they will attack Potted Plant Guy. He will be forced to get out of plant and reveal his secret identity.

Once Potted Plant Guy's secret identity was revealed, his evil powers would be destroyed.

Anyway, we hoped so.

At the very least, we could tell his mother on him.

"Hmm, I don't know, boys," Mr. Felder said. "They pull a lot. And they hate Potted Plant Guy!"

Perry and I looked at each other.

"We can handle them, sir," I said in my best Cub Scout voice.

"I guess we could give it a try some time," Mr. Felder said doubtfully.

"How about now?" I asked.

I think I sounded too eager because Mr. Felder narrowed his eyes at me.

In the end, though, he got the leashes and the little blue poop bags.

"Careful in the elevator," he warned as he handed us the leashes. "Lola and Noodle can be very playful if another dog walks in."

So wouldn't you know it, but a dog did walk in. A big, scary-looking dog. The sort of dog people name Ripper. In a flash those two dumb poodles went for Ripper. The whole way down, Lola and Noodle were out of their minds. They

were barking and snapping, and their spit was flying everywhere. Ripper gave it right back, too. By the time we reached the lobby, Ripper's owner was looking pretty fried. But Perry and I were smiling.

You know why?

Because if that was Lola and Noodle being "playful," imagine what they'd do when they saw Potted Plant Guy.

Okay, just so you don't think we were being *totally* cruel, Lola and Noodle were each about the size of a Pillow Pet. We didn't think they'd be able to kill Potted Plant Guy or anything, but they sure as heck could make him leave the potted plant pretty fast.

Cat and Boris were waiting for us down by the mailboxes in the lobby, just like we had planned.

"Ready?" Perry asked them.

They looked at the crazy barking beasts we were holding. And they smiled.

"Ready," they said.

Julius watched us coming. He must have known something funny was going on. He straightened up to his full height and tried to block our way. But he was no match for those dogs. With a quick dart to the right, they shot past him, dragging us behind them.

There was Potted Plant Guy! I could see his beady eyes staring at us between the leaves.

He didn't look scared. In fact, his eyes suddenly squinted up, like he was smiling.

"Ready, set . . ." Perry said to us. "RELEASE THE WEAPONS!"

Then we dropped the leashes.

You know that moment when you are at the very top of a roller coaster? When the next few seconds are going to be a mix of terror and delight? That's exactly how I felt right then.

The dogs shot across the lobby.

Together they leapt through the air, teeth bared.

And they landed directly on Ripper, whose owner had stopped to talk to someone in the lobby.

What happened next is hard to say. It was just like a dogfight in TV cartoons where there's this blurry ball of fur and spit and those curvy cartoon action lines. You couldn't tell who was winning either. Ripper made a quick lunge, pulling the leash right out of his owner's hands. Julius moved in and tried to grab the leash back. But I tell you, those dogs had lost their marbles! Julius finally gave up when Noodle ripped the sleeve of his doorman uniform. Then Julius gave us a *really* dirty look.

People started collecting in the lobby now, watching the fight. But no one knew what to do.

It didn't seem like things could get any worse.

So of course they did.

My mom walked through the lobby doors, carrying groceries. When she saw what was going on, she didn't hesitate. She reached right into her grocery bag and pulled out a can of Cheez Whiz. Let me tell you, she was like one of those old-time cowboys. *Ka-POW!* She whipped off the top of the can. *Ka-BAM!* She started spraying those dogs with Cheez Whiz! It stopped the fighting right away. The dogs looked totally shocked. There was Cheez Whiz everywhere, but there was an especially big glob of it right on top of Ripper's nose. Then Lola and Noodle did the most amazing thing. They started licking Ripper's nose. Their tails began to wag. Ripper looked a little nervous, but then his tail wagged, too.

People oohed and aahed.

“Woo-hoo, *Mom*!” I yelled.

That was a mistake.

She saw the leash and the poop bags in my hand. Then she saw Perry, holding the other leash and looking guilty. Mom’s eyes went all narrow and her lips got tight-looking.

Even The Biggle looked mad.

“You are in time-out, buster,” she told me as she grabbed up a poodle in each arm with no problem.

"You mean 'grounded,'" I said. "Time-out is for three-year-olds."

"And your point is?" she said.

I heard Potted Plant Guy laugh. "Heh, heh, heh." Then he stuck one hand through the leaves and held up two fingers.

Two more days until the full moon.

His evil knew no bounds.

HORRIBLE HOUNDS ACADEMY

The next morning at breakfast my mom said, "Otis, I think I know what your big problem is."

Even though I didn't like where this was going, I was sort of interested. I mean, I do have quite a few problems. I hate shirts with tight collars, for instance. And when I'm on an escalator I am afraid I'll slip and my hair will get caught between the stairs and my head will get crushed.

"The thing is," Mom said, "you have all this energy zinging around in your body and nowhere to put it. But I think I've found the perfect solution."

She handed me a flyer.

"Are you kidding?!" I cried. "Hula-hoops are for girls!"

"There's a boy right here," Mom said, pointing to the flyer.

The kid looked like someone had fed him a pound of Jolly Ranchers, stuck a hoop around him, then took a picture as he got all bonkers on the sugar rush.

My mom said that if I didn't have something to do this summer I was going to keep getting into trouble. So I *had* to take a class. This was what she called "nonnegotiable." Which basically means tough luck for me.

Gunther loved it. He was scarfing down cereal while Smoochie was lounging on the table in front of him. Now Gunther was laughing so hard, milk sprayed out of his mouth. Smoochie rolled his fat body over so he could lick the milk off the table. Yechh!

"Gunther, take that rat off the kitchen table," Mom said.

"Why? He's cleaner than Otis. And smarter."

"Off!" Mom said.

Gunther put Smoochie on his head.

"Don't worry, Otis," Gunther said. "Hula-hoops will give you nice womanly hips to help keep your pants up." Then he gave me a splinky. In case you don't know what that is, here is an illustration:

Splinky Instructions: Grab the elastic waist snaps on a skinny kid's pants, stretch them out as far as you can, then let go!

But then my mom said to him, "And you're coming with us, Gunther. There's a Teen Social Club in the same building. You can make new friends while Otis Hula-hoops."

Well, Gunther started wailing about that one. If there's one thing Gunther can't stand it's other people. But Mom didn't care. One hour later we were still grumbling as we headed out the door to sign up for the classes.

But things worked out MUCH better than I thought. Because taped above the elevator buttons was a new Tidwell Tidbit.

Do You Have A BAD Dog?

Enroll them in Horrible Hounds Academy. Mrs. Dooda will whip your little troublemaker into shape. (She doesn't use whips, but she does use Cheez Whiz.) Just visit her in apartment 35B. And call her Kiki. She likes that.

Miss Yabby

"Kiki?" my mother said. "But my name is Linda."

At that very moment, the elevator door opened and who should walk out but Ripper and his owner. Ripper must have remembered me because he started barking at me right away.

his owner cried.

"Just who I was looking for! I want to enroll my dog in Horrible Hounds Academy."

My mom started to tell her that there was no such thing as Horrible Hounds Academy when the elevator door opened again. A lady with a cocker spaniel stepped out.

she said.

There was so much barking in the hallway now that the Stink Eye lady poked her head out of the door and gave my mother the Stink Eye.

My mother's not as used to it as I am.

"All right," Mom said to the dog owners, "come inside my apartment and let's discuss this."

So the Tidwell Tidbit saved the day for both Gunther and me. Gunther ran back to his room and locked himself in with Smoochie and his cell phone. I ran over to Perry's apartment to figure out a new Kibosh. Tomorrow night was the full moon. I was running out of time.

ATTACK OF THE GRIM FUGLES

"Otis!" Perry said, a big smile on his face. He held up his hand for a high five. "We thought you'd be in time-out for a month."

"Grounded," I reminded him, giving him the five. "Anyway, we have to figure out The Kibosh."

"Don't worry. We're already working on it," Perry said. "But in the meantime, Dad wanted us to test out a new party game. Want to help?"

I know, I know. The Fluffinator didn't exactly turn out well for me. But I figured it was

in my own best interest to stay out of my apartment now, in case Mom started in on the Hula-hoop thing again.

In the living room, Mr. Hooper was kneeling by a battered old box filled with shredded paper. On the outside of the box were the words "Grim Fugles."

"What do the instructions say, Boris?" Mr. Hooper asked.

Boris stared down at the booklet he was holding. "Loogit dreeber foogle."

Mr. Hooper gave Boris a worried look. "Are you coming down with a cold?"

"That's what it says here." Boris shook

the booklet. "It's like it's written in a different language."

Cat snatched the paper out of Boris's hands and looked at it.

"That's because it *is* written in a different language," she said. Then she looked up at Mr. Hooper sternly. "Where did you get this game from?" she asked him.

"Um." Mr. Hooper turned all kinds of red.

"From the back of someone's truck for ten dollars?" Cat demanded.

"No, of course not!" Mr. Hooper said. "It was four dollars. And I got it from a very nice man. On the subway platform."

"By any chance, was he also selling Cheez Doodles dressed up as people?" I asked.

"Why yes! Yes he was." Mr. Hooper brightened right up.

At that moment Peaches trotted into the room. Well, to be honest, Peaches' aroma trotted in first, followed by Peaches. Cat and Boris covered their noses. Perry and his dad acted like nothing was wrong. I guess it's like not being able to smell your own bad breath because you're always around it. I didn't cover my nose either, but that was because I felt bad for Peaches. I know he's just a horse, but I kept imagining how it would feel to have everyone cover their noses when you walked into a room.

Okay, I'll level with you. I know *exactly* what it feels like. When I was in the first grade people

used to do the same thing to me when I walked into a room. The doctor said that drinking milk gave me "bottom burps." She actually called it that! I nearly died of embarrassment. Anyway, that made me feel very sympathetic to Peaches. I think he appreciated it, too, because he stuck his face in my armpit and kept it there.

Or maybe he was just trying to cover his own nose.

Mr. Hooper reached into the battered old box, which seemed pretty brave to me. Who knew what sort of disgusting thing might be in there? He dug through the shredded paper and pulled out a plastic green bird with an orange baseball cap glued to its head. After digging around some more, he pulled out three more birds, just like the first one but with different-colored baseball caps. The last thing he pulled out was a remote control.

He started fiddling with the remote control, messing around with the buttons and levers. All of a sudden the birds' wings started flapping. All four of them flew up to the ceiling and started circling over our heads.

"Now this looks like fun!" Mr. Hooper said.

But there was something creepy about it. The birds were making these rumbling noises.

"Make them come down, Mr. Hooper," Boris said nervously.

Mr. Hooper started pushing at the levers again. But the birds didn't come down. Instead the rumbling got louder. Then there was a clicking sound. I looked up to see that a little trapdoor had opened near each of the birds' rear ends.

You know those movies where kids fight off scary monsters with toothpaste, gasoline, and their mom's hair spray?

We're not those kinds of kids.

We ran.

POO BOMBS

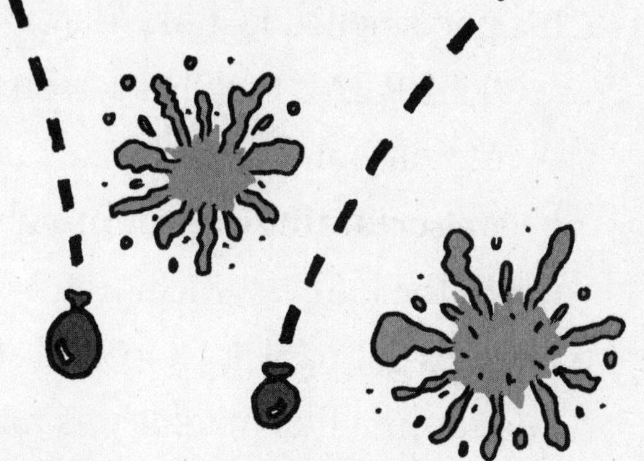

Mr. Hooper got his four dollars' worth with the Grim Fugles. Boy, those things could really fly!

They followed us through the apartment and out into the hallway. That was when one of them began to drop little white things out of its trapdoor. They looked like tiny white balloons. *SPLAT!!!* The balloons hit us, and this gooey yellowy-white stuff exploded all over the

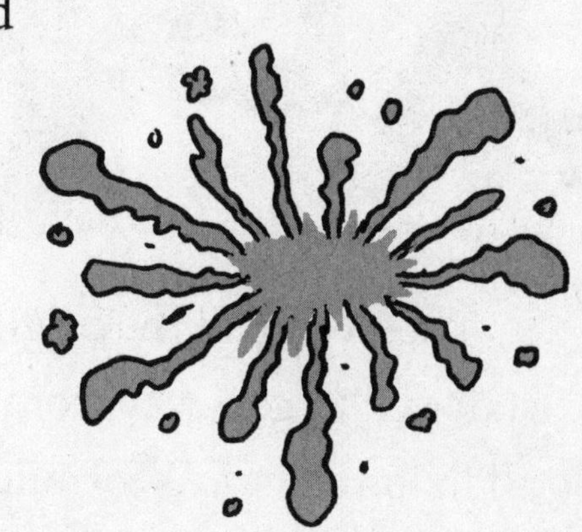

place. And this is the disgusting part. I think the balloons might have been filled with actual bird poo. No kidding. I had a canary once and his poo smelled just like that.

"IT'S REAL POO!" I screamed.

At that point a riot broke out. Everyone began screaming and running in all directions down the hallway, including Mr. Hooper. Peaches got panicky, too, and started galloping and tooting like mad. It was total chaos!

Then Cat had the bright idea to run into the stairwell to get away from the poo bombs. We all followed her. We would have escaped, too, but when Peaches got to the door, he just stood there, holding the door open, like he wasn't sure what to do. By the time Peaches decided he was going to stay right in the hallway, those birds had already flown into the stairwell. We were pounding down the stairs as fast as we could, but those birds just followed us. Every few seconds they'd drop another load of poo bombs. We were dripping with the revolting stuff and slipping on it as we ran. Boris had it the worst though.

The more he tried to wipe it off his thick hair, the more he smeared it in, until it was all white and caked up in sticky clumps. He looked like my grandmother before we had to put her in the nursing home.

On the twenty-fifth floor, Mr. Hooper did something heroic. He stopped running and faced the Grim Fugles dead-on. Jumping up in the air, he swatted at them with the remote control. He did manage to knock one against the wall. It made a *phflooofisssss* sound, then fell to the floor.

The problem was, this only seemed to make the other Grim Fugles really mad. Now they were in a frenzy, flying at Mr. Hooper's head and dropping poo bombs twice as fast.

That was when I heard a little voice in my head. It said:

"You know what to doodle-do, Otis."

And guess what?

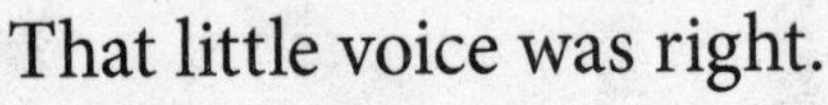

That little voice was right.

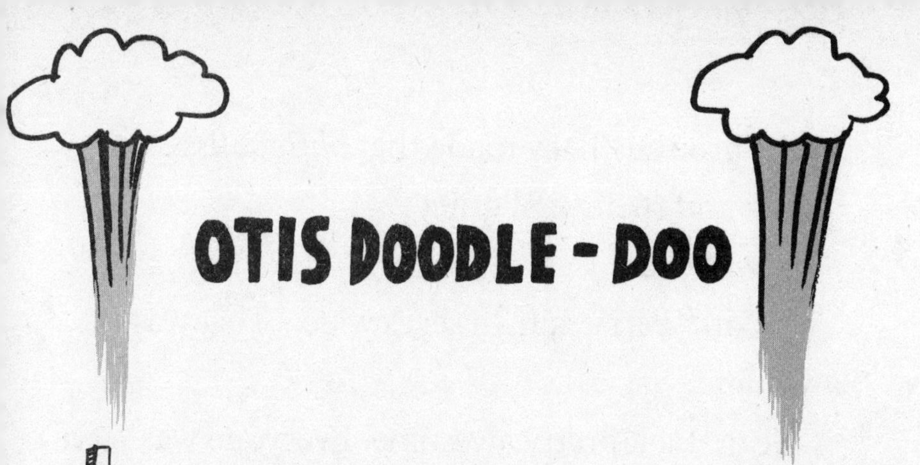

OTIS DOODLE-DOO

In a flash I grabbed the remote control out of Mr. Hooper's hands, threw it down, and started stomping on it. Everyone looked at me like I had gone berserk.. I stomped until the plastic cover cracked open. I just kept stomping. Finally, the birds stopped flapping their wings and crashed

to the ground. They made that *phflooofisssss* sound and then went quiet.

It was over.

"Wow," Perry said, his eyes wide. "That was . . . awesome."

Yeah, I felt pretty awesome. Everyone was staring at me. Even Cat looked impressed.

"How did you think to do that, Otis?" Mr. Hooper asked.

"It just came to me," I said.

Which was a big fat lie.

The real reason I broke the remote control was because of my secret identity. Otis Doodle-Doo.

Remember in the beginning I said something bad had happened to me back in Hog's Head? And that I wasn't sure I wanted to tell you what it was?

Well, since you just saw a picture of me with poo on my head, I might as well just tell you everything.

Here's what happened:

I had a giant stuffed chicken named Uncle Clucky. He was blue with big googly eyes. And . . . I'm just going to say it. I loved Uncle Clucky. I had had him since I was a baby and he was all crusty, but I didn't care. I slept with him every night, even though Gunther made fun of me. One day, a few weeks before we were going

to move to New York City, I was messing around with a motor from one of my Lego sets. I decided to do something fun with Uncle Clucky. I wired up the motor to my skateboard. Then I tied Uncle Clucky to the skateboard and went outside and put the skateboard on the sidewalk. I walked ahead of it a few yards. Then I turned on my remote control. Right away Uncle Clucky started zooming down the street toward me. I tried to slow him down with the remote control but it didn't work. I couldn't even make him stop. He was coming at me crazy fast. He was swaying back and forth on the skateboard, and his googly eyes were bouncing all over the place. He looked like he'd been taken over by a demon. A giant blue chicken demon. It freaked me out so much that I started to run. I ran down

the entire street followed by a chicken on a skateboard. It's a very long street. With lots of kids.

Plus I think I may have been screaming a little.

Finally I threw the remote control into the road where a car ran over it and smashed it. That was when Uncle Clucky stopped. After I calmed down, I took a look at the motor and saw that the wiring had been all wrong. It was my fault that Uncle Clucky chased me.

All the kids in the neighborhood told everyone at school that I had been scared of a stuffed chicken.

After that, everyone at school started to call me Otis Doodle-Doo. Which is actually dumb because Uncle Clucky was a chicken, not a rooster.

But you know what? I never felt the same about Uncle Clucky after that.

Anyway, that's how I knew what to do about the Grim Fugles. The remote control had been wired all wrong, just like Uncle Clucky's.

Now Cat was staring at me through her red-rimmed glasses.

I frowned at her.

"What?" I asked.

"Nothing," she said. "I was just thinking that you might not be such a schmo after all."

I'm not sure what a schmo is. But I think she might have given me a compliment.

PLAN B (FOR BAD)

We were all so smelly and sticky from the poo bombs that we had to go home and clean up. After that we would meet back in Cat's apartment to figure out what to do about The Kibosh.

But surprise, surprise! On our apartment door was a sign that said:

I walked into the apartment and was instantly mobbed by a pack of jumping, barking dogs.

"For the hundredth time, SHUT UP!" Gunther yelled from his room.

My mother came running down the hall, holding this big mirror. She held the mirror up in front of those crazy dogs and said, "Look at yourselves!! Just *look*!! Aren't you ashamed?!!"

The dogs looked. They got quiet and stared at their reflections. Some of them wagged their tails at the mirror. Noodle tried to walk into it and cracked his head on the mirror.

"You look ridiculous," my mother continued sternly.

"Totally," I agreed. "Especially you," I said, pointing at Noodle.

"I was talking to *you*, Otis," my mother said, staring at the yellowy-white splotches all over me. "What is that stuff? Is that bird poo? You look like that statue of the mayor in the park back in Hog's Head."

And then, as if to prove Mom's point, Noodle whizzed on me.

* * *

After I was all scrubbed up, I tried to leave the apartment. It wasn't easy. The dogs were jumping all over me and going nutso again. Mom rushed over with this box of bone-shaped dog biscuits. I thought she was going to bribe them with the biscuits. Instead she shook the box in their faces. It made a loud rattley sound and they all shut up and looked at her.

"Sit!" she told them.

And you know what? They did.

Then she pulled a soy wiener out of her pocket and gave them each a piece. Apparently, dogs will do anything for soy wieners. Which proves my theory that soy wieners are actually dog food in a tube.

I headed over to Cat's apartment. Two of the mini Cats, Lucy and Linus, opened the door.

"Where's Hobbes?" I asked, just to be friendly.

Lucy and Linus snickered, then ran away.

I've said it before and I'll say it again: Little kids are weird. If you asked a grown-up a question and they snickered and ran away, you'd probably think they escaped from a mental hospital.

In Cat's room, Perry, Boris, and Cat were kneeling by a big pet carrier.

"You all right in there?" Cat said to the pet carrier.

A little grunt came out of the carrier.

"What's going on, guys?" I asked.

"What's going on is Plan B," Cat said.

"We figured out how to put The Kibosh on Potted Plant Guy," Perry said.

"Without me?" I admit this hurt my feelings.

"No tears, Slimderella," Boris said, putting his arm around me.

"I'm not crying," I said.

"Yeah? Then what's that wet stuff on your eyeballs?" he said.

"Eyeball juice." I shook Boris's arm off me and knelt down to look in the pet carrier. Hobbes was smooshed in there and was staring back at me.

"How is Hobbes in a pet carrier going to put The Kibosh on Potted Plant Guy?" I asked.

"Hobbes is going to be our spy," Perry explained. "We're going to put the carrier in the lobby and leave it there. And when Potted Plant Guy gets up to go to the bathroom or have lunch, *Bang*! Hobbes will see who he is."

I looked at Hobbes crammed in the carrier.

You know when someone has an idea that is sooo good, you wish you had thought of it yourself?

This wasn't one of those ideas.

EXTREME SOUR SMARTIES

We all marched into the lobby, past Julius and Potted Plant Guy. Boris was in front, holding Hobbes in the pet carrier.

"What's this?" Julius narrowed his eyes at us suspiciously.

"This cat is very sick," Boris told Julius. He put the carrier down in the far corner of the lobby. "Don't let anyone go near it."

"Yeah? What's wrong with the cat?" Julius asked.

Boris turned all kinds of colors. I guess he hadn't thought things through very well. Then he muttered, "Halitosis."

Julius frowned. "Halitosis is just bad breath."

"Bunions," Boris tried again.

"That's what old ladies get on their feet," Julius said.

Thankfully Cat stepped up and said, "Tuffy has a very contagious case of ringworm. We can't have her near our other cats. The vet will come by in a few hours to pick her up."

Julius made a *hmmph* sound, like he wasn't really buying it. But then he turned back to the door and did his doorman thing again. So it seemed like Plan B was going to work after all.

We made little thumbs-up signs to each other, then started to leave.

That was when Potted Plant Guy shouted, “Who wants Extreme Sour Smarties?!”

Hobbes unlatched the cage door, crawled out, and ran to Potted Plant Guy for some Extreme Sour Smarties.

Julius rolled his eyes.

I looked over at Potted Plant Guy. His evil genius eyes glinted back at me.

"Big deal! That wasn't so clever," I told him. "I mean, who DOESN'T want Extreme Sour Smarties?"

His hand pushed through the leaves, and he held up one finger. I knew what it meant.

One more day before the full moon.

RANCH-FLAVORED FAMILY FUN

I needed to take my mind off what was going to happen to me tomorrow. So I went back home and built a Lego spaceship. That calmed me right down. Then Dad came home and we sat on the couch with a bag of family-fun-sized ranch-flavored Fritos and watched *Jeopardy!* Dad hardly ever knows any of the answers,

but once in a while he gets one right. It's usually questions like, "The manager of the railway on

Thomas the Tank Engine." And Dad jumps up and yells, "Who is Sir Topham Hatt!"

Then Dad says, "I should be on this show. Darn straight, I should."

I always get a kick out of that.

Dad wasn't too happy about the whole Horrible Hounds Academy, though. Especially since Mom agreed to have one of the dogs *stay*

at our house. She said it was because the dog, a tubby little terrier named Rodney, needed extra attention. I think it was because its owner needed a break from that fruitcake animal.

First of all, Rodney kept licking the same spot on the living-room rug over and over and over again.

Slurp, slurp, slurp!

Dad finally screamed,

Rodney looked at Dad. Then he waddled over to the couch and started licking Dad's pants.

Mom was downstairs in the laundry room, and I felt sorry for Dad. Plus, I didn't want him to nix the whole Horrible Hounds Academy because it distracted Mom from putting me in some dumb class. So I grabbed Rodney by the collar and I dragged him to Gunther's room. Gunther was on the phone with Pandora, and they were having one of their silent picking sessions. I figured Rodney and Gunther and Pandora could all have a nice Pick and Lick party. But in a few minutes Gunther came storming out of his room. Rodney was licking Smoochie's cage, and Gunther said he couldn't concentrate with all the slobbering noise.

I guess picking your pimples takes more focus than you'd think.

So I was stuck with the dingbat dog. I put him in my room. But then he started licking the light socket. I happen to know from personal experience that licking light sockets is not a good idea. I decided I'd better distract him before he fried himself. I ran to the kitchen to get some soy wieners, but we had run out of them. Instead, I grabbed a bunch of bone-shaped dog biscuits and shoved them in my pocket. But when I held one out for Rodney, he just looked at it, then went back to licking the light socket.

I decided to try something else. I went into Gunther's room. He was still holding the phone to his ear and picking away. He didn't even notice when I grabbed Smoochie's cage and brought it into my room. When Rodney saw it, he forgot all about the light socket and started licking the cage. Smoochie just sat there, all flabby and dopey, and watched him. It struck me that Smoochie was like the rat version of Rodney. They were both so blahhh. If ever there were two animals that needed some exercise, it was these two.

Suddenly I had a great idea. I closed my bedroom door. Then I took the lid off Smoochie's cage, picked him up, and put him on the floor. I figured I'd let Rodney chase Smoochie around the room for a while. It would bring a little excitement into their sad, flabby lives. But wouldn't you know it, the two of them just sat there staring at each other!

That's when I had another brilliant idea. I took one of the dog biscuits out of my pocket and tied it to Smoochie's tail with a string. Now

Rodney perked up a little. He started licking the biscuit. Smoochie wasn't too happy about that, so he turned around and attacked Rodney. No kidding. That rat suddenly turned into a pudgy pro-wrestling star! He was biting and squeaking and jumping all over Rodney. Rodney just yelped and spun in circles.

I started screaming, "Stop, stop, STOP!"

And I might have been spinning in circles, too.

I'm not good in a crisis.

"What's all the hoopla?" Dad said as he came into my room.

That was when Smoochie made a beeline for the door.

Now here comes the part of this story that is rated PG-13. Which means if you are the sensitive type, you should skip to the next chapter.

If you do decide to keep reading, please remember this important fact:

Rats usually live about three years.

Smoochie was two and a half.

Smoochie scurried into the living room. We rushed after him. At first, we thought we had lost him. But then we saw the family-fun-sized bag of ranch-flavored Fritos start to move. He had run into the bag and couldn't find his way back out again (so much for Gunther's theory about Smoochie being smarter than me). I made a lunge for the bag, but it toppled off the couch just as Smoochie tore a hole in one end. He was so fat that only his head and front paws fit through the hole. I guess he must have panicked or something because he ran out the open balcony door with the Fritos bag dragging behind him and . . .

Well, the last thing we saw was a family-fun-sized bag of Fritos flying off the edge of the balcony.

By the time Dad and I ran out to the balcony, Smoochie was gone.

"Poor little guy," Dad said, shaking his head. "Poor Smoochers."

I'm not going to lie to you. I never liked that rat. But I felt really terrible. What a way to go—flying through the air in a Fritos bag.

Still, I tried to look on the bright side. Now I knew how I was going to break all of my bones.

Gunther was going to do it for me once he found out what happened to Smoochie.

LUCKY BREAK

I was wrong. Gunther didn't break all of my bones. The only thing he did was cry. It made me feel so bad that I wished he would have broken my bones instead. And he has such a big head, it was like watching someone cry through

a zoom lens. I told him I'd buy him a new rat. I had some money I was saving up to get this cool Lego race-car set.

"I don't want another rat!" he wailed. "There's no other rat like Smoochie!"

I had to agree with him. Most other rats are probably a lot better than Smoochie.

But I didn't say that. It would have been inappropriate. Also, I really wanted that Lego race-car set.

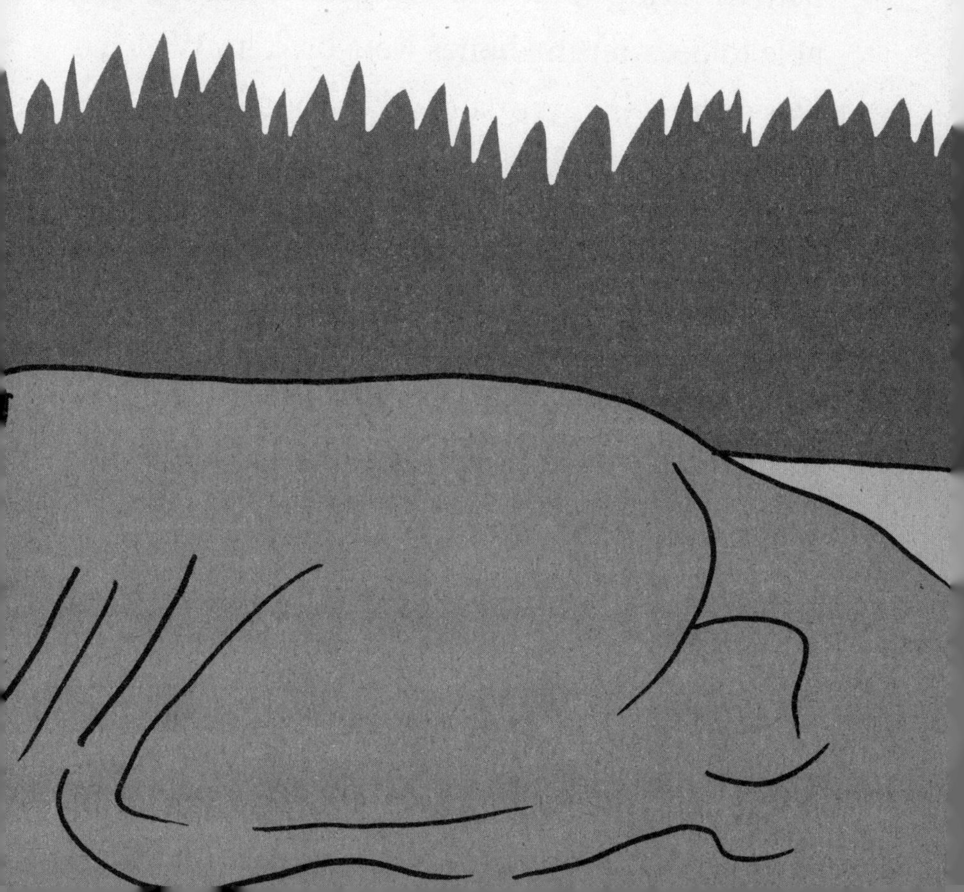

FRESH-BAKED CINNAMON BUNS

It's a funny thing about bones. You don't really notice them until the day they are all supposed to break. The next morning, I lay in bed, thinking about the things I wouldn't be able to do after my bones were broken. Which was everything. Worst of all, I wouldn't be able to build with Legos. How would I survive?!

But then I had a bright idea. If I just stayed in my bed all day long and didn't do a single thing, how could I break my bones? It would be impossible. And by tomorrow the curse would be over. It was so simple!

So I just lay there.

After about seven minutes, I discovered it is very hard to lie in your bed all day and do nothing. Also, I was hungry.

I yelled for my mother. I had to yell about a hundred times before she came. When she opened my door, five dogs rushed in ahead of her and pounced on me.

"Gahhh! Get these dogs off me before they break my bones!" I shrieked.

"Don't be such a drama queen," my mother said. Then she growled at all the dogs and bared her teeth. No kidding. The dogs ran off my bed and out the door.

"Okay, Otis," she said, "what do you want?"

"Um." She made me a little nervous after that growling thing. I wondered if those crazy dogs were rubbing off on her. If she started licking light sockets, I was going to call the SPCA for advice.

"Well?" she said.

"Could you bring me some breakfast?" I asked politely.

She looked at me like she was about to bare her teeth again. "Why? Are your legs broken?" she demanded.

"Duh! That's just the point!" I said. "I'm trying NOT to break them!"

Actually I said this after she left and closed the door.

Just when it was becoming clear that I was going to starve in my bed, Perry walked into my room.

"Perry!" I cried. "Just in time! Listen, go tell my mother you want some cereal."

I figured he stood a better chance with Mom than I did.

"Why?" Perry asked.

"Because I'm staying in my bed all day so that I don't break my bones."

Perry frowned. "That won't work," he said.

"Sure it will."

Perry shook his head. "We couldn't put The Kibosh on Potted Plant Guy. Your bones are going to break no matter what you do." He picked up the pair of jeans that were lying on the floor and handed them to me. "Instead of just lying here all day, why don't you come with us on The Big Green Party Machine? We need some help. And at least you'll have fun while you're waiting for your bones to break."

That made sense.

Plus I *really* wanted to ride on The Big Green Party Machine.

* * *

By the time I got dressed and ate three bowls of cereal, Mr. Hooper, Perry, Cat, and Boris were all out in the hall, getting ready to leave.

Mr. Hooper was pushing this weird-looking chair on wheels. It had a huge fan attached to the back of it. Cat was dressed as an angry clown, and Perry was dressed as a happy clown.

Even Peaches was dressed up in a red coat with a hole cut out for his tail.

"What are *you* supposed to be?" I asked Boris.

He had drawn a curly mustache above his lip and he wore an orange glow stick around his head.

"I'm the magician, what do you think?" he said, as though it were obvious.

“Yeah?” I said. “What kind of tricks do you do?”

“I can flip my eyelids backward,” Boris said. He did it. It was disgusting.

“That’s not a magic trick,” I told him.

"Big deal," I said.

"It IS a big deal," Boris said. "Go on. Try and lick your elbow."

I tried and you know what? I couldn't. I bet you can't either. Go on and try. I'll wait.

See? Isn't that weird?

"So what am I supposed to do at the party?" I asked.

"You can be a clown, too," Perry said. "We'll fix you up on the bus."

I liked the idea of that. I'd always wanted to wear those big, floppy shoes.

Suddenly I saw Peaches start to lift his tail.

"Code red, code red!" I cried. "Peaches is going to blow!!"

No one put their hands over their noses. In fact, they were smiling.

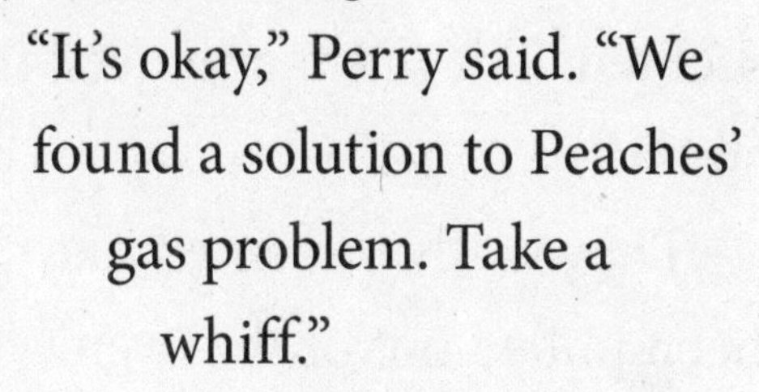

"It's okay," Perry said. "We found a solution to Peaches' gas problem. Take a whiff."

I took one careful sniff.

It smelled like cinnamon buns. No kidding. Fresh cinnamon buns, all sugary and sweet. I smiled.

"Told you," Perry said.

"But . . . how did you do that?" I asked.

"It was my idea," Cat said. She lifted the back of Peaches' red coat. Two white discs were taped onto either side of his rear end.

"Air fresheners," she said. "Cinnamon-bun scented. The warmer it gets, the stronger they smell."

They really did smell like the buns had just been pulled out of the oven.

"Brilliant!" I said.

Cat looked pleased.

So did Peaches. It must be nice for him to get a break from his own stench once in a while.

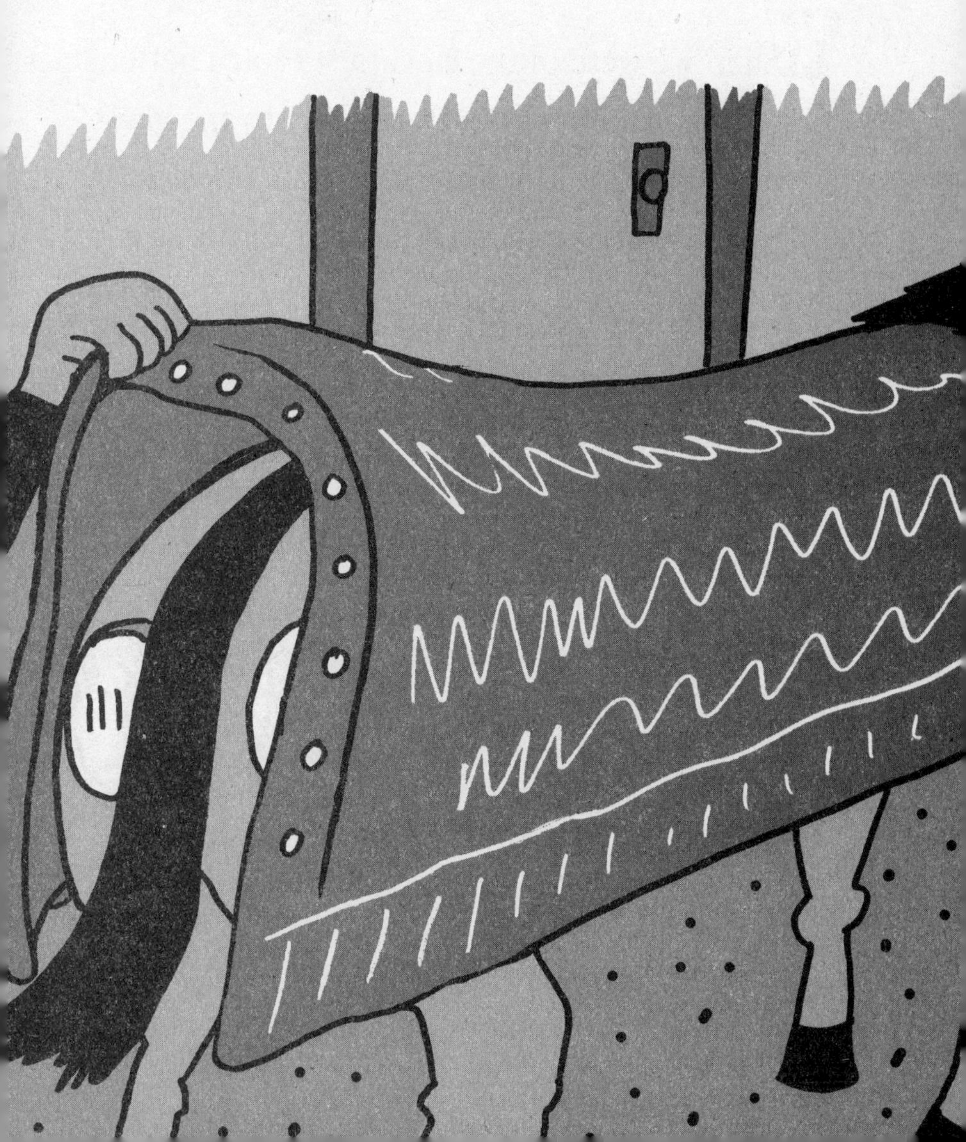

POTTY-MOBILE

When we were in the elevator I took a better look at Mr. Hooper's contraption with the giant fan attached to it. It looked like a tall wheelchair, only there was a hole in the middle of the seat.

I stared.

I squinted.

Finally I said, MR. HOOPER, IS THAT WHAT I THINK IT IS?

Mr. Hooper cleared his throat and started turning funny colors.

Then he said, "It's a portable commode."

"It's a toilet on wheels," I said.

"That's another name for it," he admitted.

"We got it for my grandfather when he was sick," Perry said.

"But why are you bringing it to a kid's birthday party?" I asked.

"Well," Mr. Hooper explained, "the Fluffinator looked like it wouldn't work out, and then of course the Grim Fugles . . . well, that was a disaster. So we had to do something. Perry and I rigged up this old toilet so that it's motorized. I thought it would be fun for the kids. I put in a seat belt. And you can steer it with this bar."

It actually did look like fun.

"How fast can it go?" I asked.

The elevator dinged as we slowed down for the lobby.

"I'll show you," Boris said. He hopped on the toilet, and as the elevator door opened, he flipped a switch by the fan. It started to whir and the toilet glided out of the elevator.

"Cool!" I said.

The fan began to pick up some speed. So did the toilet.

"Step on the pedal by your left foot to slow down, Boris!" Mr. Hooper called to him.

But Boris didn't seem to hear. He was zipping down the lobby faster and faster. His steering wasn't too great, either. He nearly flattened

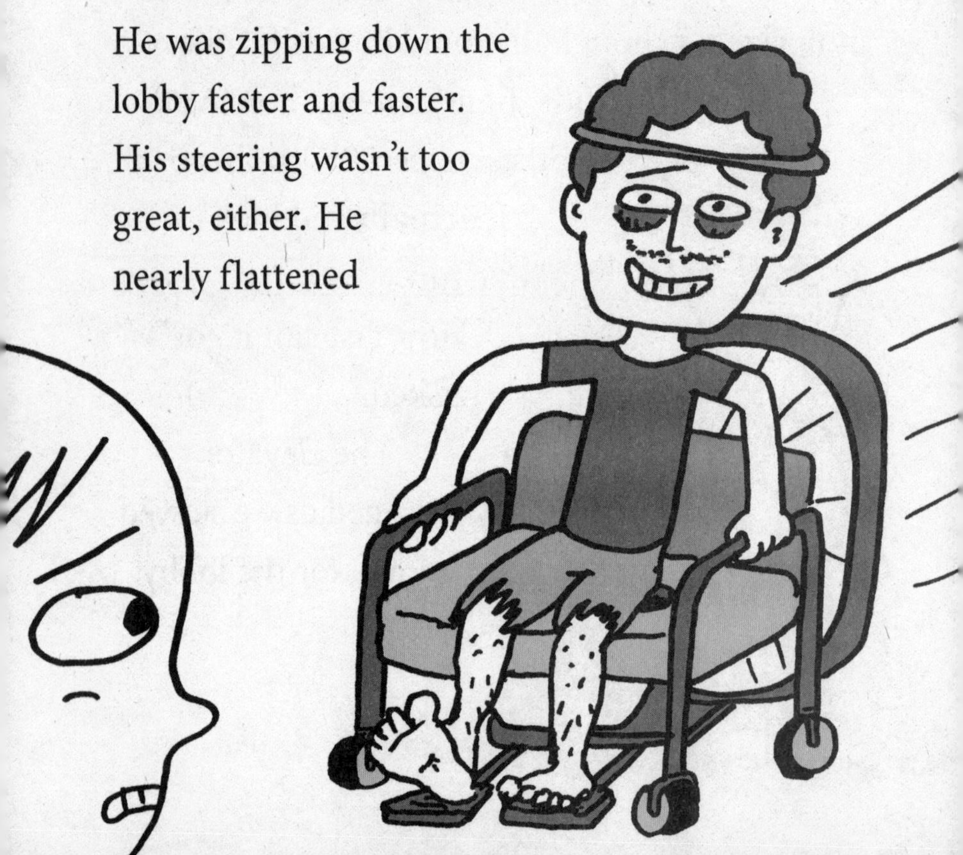

some lady, but she jumped away just in time. The fan was blowing so hard that her hat flew right off her head.

It was when Boris was just a few feet away from Potted Plant Guy that I realized something. The fan was going to blow the leaves of that plant all over the place. In another

few seconds, everyone in the lobby was going to find out who Potted Plant Guy was.

I knew he had cursed me and everything. And that we had been trying to figure out who he was. But at that moment I suddenly thought about Legos. I thought about the way they make me feel whenever I freak out about something. How they calm me down. How the *snap-snap* sound of the bricks fitting together makes me feel good again, even if people are calling me things like Otis Chewbacca Chunks and Otis Doodle-Doo.

And I suddenly wondered if that's how Potted Plant Guy felt about his plant.

I started running. The toilet was moving so fast, and the wind from the fan was blowing back at me, but I kept running.

"Stop, Boris!" I yelled.

Julius also saw what was about to happen. He started running, but he was too far away. It was up to me.

Sometimes having Twizzler legs comes in handy.

I leapt into the air and landed on the edge of the pot. Just as the fan was about to reach Potted Plant Guy I squatted down and spread my arms wide. The fan blew the leaves this way and that but I kept Potted Plant Guy hidden behind me.

Boris, Cat, and Perry all stared at me like I was crazy.

Julius was smiling.

The lady with the hat sniffed the air and said, "Who's baking cinnamon buns?"

Behind me, I felt a tug on my shirt, and Potted Plant Guy said, "Thanks."

"No problem," I replied.

I thought for a minute. "So does this mean I won't break all my bones?" I asked.

"Oh, you'll still break them," Potted Plant Guy said. "But I promise that you won't feel a thing."

THE BIG GREEN PARTY MACHINE

The Big Green Party Machine was just a dented old school bus that was painted green. We all sat in the way back. Of course, the first thing Boris, Cat, and Perry wanted to know was why I did what I did for Potted Plant Guy.

“I’ve got my reasons,” I said.

OTIS DOODA, YOU ARE ONE WEIRD KID Perry said.

But he smiled a little when he said it, so I didn't mind.

"Hey," I said, "where's my clown outfit?"

I was looking forward to wearing that thing. I hoped it came with one of those plastic flowers that squirted water in people's faces.

"We don't have an outfit for you," Cat said. "But we do have a wig." She took this rainbow-colored Afro wig out of a bag and stuck it on my head.

"Now keep still," she told me as she pulled out a makeup kit. "I'm going to paint your face."

The bus was really bouncy. Cat's hand kept jerking around as she put on the clown makeup. I could tell by the expressions on Perry's and Boris's faces that things weren't going very well.

"Done!" she said and handed me a little mirror.

I looked like one of those nutty old ladies who put their lipstick on all lopsided and wear pink circles on their cheeks.

Finally we pulled up to this nice house in New Jersey. There were all these little kids on the front lawn and the trees had balloons and streamers in them. The kids got really excited when they saw the bus. The grown-ups didn't look too happy though. I guess they had expected something better than a beat-up old green school bus.

When we brought out the Potty-Mobile, they looked even more unhappy.

Then we took Peaches off the bus. The kids went berserk. You'd think they'd never seen a horse before. Mr. Hooper put a little saddle on Peaches, over the red coat so no one could see the air fresheners. It was my job to lead Peaches around the front lawn while the kids rode on him.

One kid kept smiling at me. It made me feel pretty good. I guess I'm just naturally good with kids, I thought to myself. But when I put him on Peaches he said to me, "Nana, why are you wearing that funny wig?"

I said, annoyed.

"And if your nana looks like *this,* I feel sorry for you, I really do."

That made the kid start crying his head off.

Other than that, things were going pretty well. Boris was doing his repulsive eyelid trick.

Perry was juggling tennis balls. He really could juggle, too! And Cat was making balloon animals. Only all her animals looked like swords, so the kids started smacking each other over the heads with them until the grown-ups took them away.

The big hit of the party, though, was the Potty-Mobile. The kids loved that thing! Mr. Hooper ran alongside it and made sure that they didn't crash. But after a half hour, the fan busted and the Potty-Mobile wouldn't move anymore.

“What am I going to do?” Mr. Hooper whispered to us in a panicky voice. “There’s still another hour left to this party.”

“We can hook Peaches up to the toilet,” I suggested. “He can pull it.”

Everyone thought that was a great idea. We tied Peaches’ lead rope to the toilet, and guess what? The kids thought that the Horse-Drawn Potty was even better than the Potty-Mobile.

I was feeling pretty proud of myself for that idea.

Right up until the moment when I noticed a white disc on the ground.

“Uh-oh,” Perry said. He’d seen it, too.

The next minute, another white disc fell out from under Peaches’ red coat.

“The air fresheners!” I whispered.

“I know!” Perry whispered back.

I looked at the kid riding on the toilet. If Peaches let off a booty bomb, that kid was right in the line of fire.

"Someone's got to tape those air fresheners back on Peaches fast," Cat said. "And Mr. Hooper is inside ordering the pizza."

We waited. I think we were all hoping that someone would volunteer.

"Look," Boris said, "Perry can juggle, Cat can do balloon animals, and I'm a master magician.

The only useless person here is Otis. So Otis should be the one."

"Master magician? Really, Boris?" I said. "*I'll* flip my eyelids backward, then I'll be the master magician and you can fix Peaches' problem."

"Okay, let's see you do it," Boris said.

As it turns out, I can't flip my eyelids backward.

THE CAVE OF DOOM

I picked up the air fresheners.

"Hey, how come you stopped the horse?!!" the kids in line started screaming. "That's not fair!"

I growled at them and they quieted down.

"Now listen, Otis," Perry said as he handed me a roll of tape. "You've got to get in and out of there fast. Seriously. You never know when Peaches is going to blow. Plus you have to keep the red coat on him, so people don't see what you're doing. That means there won't be a lot of fresh air in there."

Then, you know what he did? He gave me the shoulder squeeze. That's right. The same shoulder squeeze that they give people before they enter the Cave of Doom.

I took a deep breath. Then I crawled under Peaches' red coat. I sniffed.

So far, so good.

Quick as anything, I tore off a piece of tape from the roll and taped the first disk onto one of Peaches' buttocks.

Half done, Otis, half done, I gave myself a little pep talk.

I started to get the second piece of tape but it ripped funny. I had to pick at a narrow little strip to get it started again. Then the most awful thing happened.

Peaches' tail lifted up.

"Oh no, oh no, oh no!" I said. "Please, Peaches, hold it in for one more minute. Just squeeze it in. You can do it, old boy, I know you can."

He couldn't do it.

The smell hit me full in the face. Suddenly everything got blurry. I started sweating and my ears felt all clogged up. The last thing I remember was Perry screaming, "Man down, man down!"

* * *

When I came to, there was an ambulance guy leaning over me. Behind him I could see Perry, Boris, Cat, Mr. Hooper, and a bunch of little kids all staring at me. They looked horrified.

"Am I okay?" I murmured.

"That's what we're trying to find out, son," the ambulance guy said. "You fell and hit your head and the horse bolted. Then this . . . toilet ran over you. Now just keep very still."

He took a little flashlight and shone it in my eyes. Then he asked me to watch his finger as he waved it back and forth. Finally he started poking at my legs. That's when I heard a crunching sound.

My bones!

He poked my leg again.

Crunch, crunch.

But I didn't feel any pain at all.

Then I remembered what Potted Plant Guy said—that I would break all my bones, but I wouldn't feel a thing.

"My bones!" I cried. "My bones! Are they all broken?"

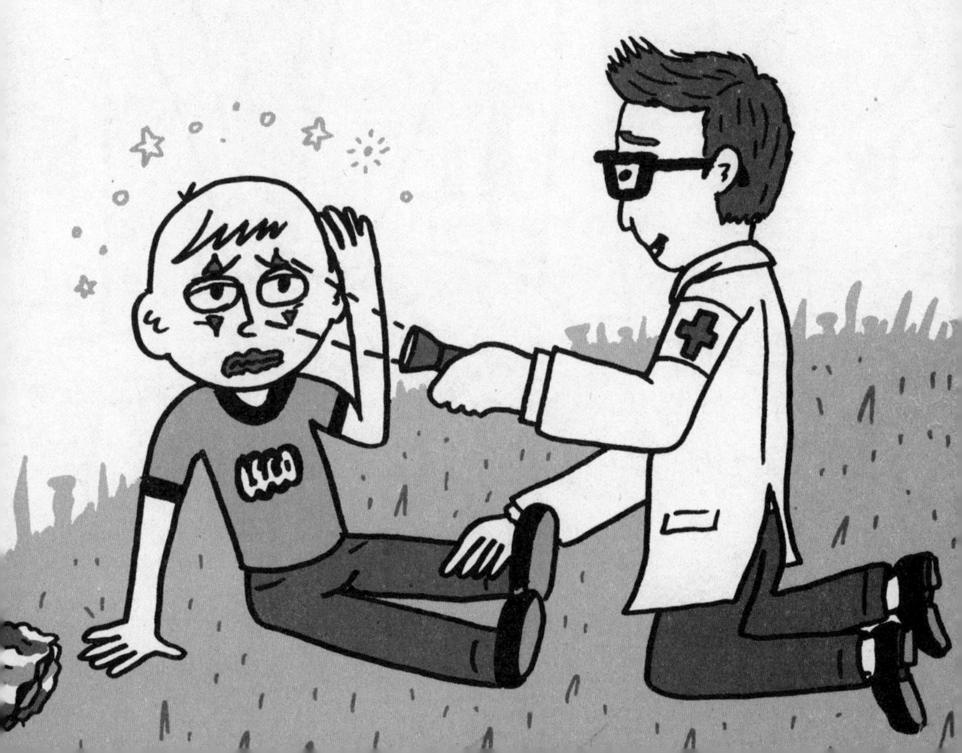

It felt like the ambulance guy was examining my leg, but I couldn't see what he was doing.

"Yep," he said. "Your bones are definitely all broken."

Then he showed me something in his hand. Something brown and crumbly.

"Are those my . . . bones?" I asked, horrified.

"Your dog bones. They were in your pocket," he said. "They're all broken. But the rest of you seems just fine."

SMOOCHIE'S FUNERAL

So the curse did come true after all. I did break all my bones. It just didn't happen the way I expected it to. Which is pretty much what happened later that day, when Mom, Dad, Gunther, and I got back from Smoochie's funeral.

Since we didn't have Smoochie to bury, we decided we'd bury his Kleenex box in Central Park. Mom made us all dress in black. We looked like a family of Applebee's waiters.

Gunther was a wreck. His eyes were all puffy. He kept saying things like, "Smoochie was one in a million." And "Where will I ever find a friend like Smoochie again?"

I heard Dad mutter,

Mom gave him the Stink Eye for that.

I was trying to act very serious, especially since Smoochie's death was really my fault. But I was so happy that all my bones weren't broken,

I just couldn't stand still. Back in the building, I was running up and down the hall and swinging my arms in circles. It just felt so great to be all in one piece! Mom poked her head out of our apartment and told me to cut it out. That's when I calmed down enough to notice that there was a new Tidwell Tidbits up.

Lost & Found

LOST: Mrs. Wexler's sense of humor. Apparently she doesn't appreciate being called "sweet cheeks."

FOUND: A rat in a Fritos bag. To claim, please see Julius.

I got all excited then. I started hopping all around and pointing at the Tidwell Tidbits, saying, "Look, look, *LOOK!*"

Dad came out and read it out loud. When he got to the part about the rat, everyone's eyes got really wide. Then *they* started hopping all around.

Right then the elevator door opened. There was a guy inside, and he watched us jumping around with this suspicious expression on his face. But when we walked into the elevator, he looked at us more closely. Then he smiled.

"Well, butter my buns!" he cried.

We were all so happy that Smoochie was okay that we smiled and said,

right back to him.

The second the elevator reached the lobby, we rushed out and ran down the lobby hall to Julius.

We were all talking to him at once.

"Slow down, Doodas," Julius said, holding up his hands. "Now, did I hear one of you say something about a rat?"

"Yes!" Gunther said. "My rat . . . Smoochie. Do you have him?"

"You mean *this* rat?" Julius reached into the pocket of his uniform and pulled out good old Smoochie, looking just as flabby and lazy as ever. I was unbelievably happy to see him. And Gunther . . . well, he grabbed Smoochie out of Julius's hand and kissed that rat right on the mouth.

I'm not even kidding.

If Pandora had seen that she'd probably pick her scalp raw.

Everyone seemed to have lost their minds with happiness. I was the only one who thought to ask the most obvious question:

"But how can Smoochie still be alive after falling off a thirty-fifth floor balcony?"

"Because," said Julius, "a family-fun-sized Fritos bag makes an excellent parachute. The wind blew him right into Mrs. Wexler's window."

"Strange," Mom said.

Julius smiled at me, a wide flash of a smile.

"Strange but true," he said.

⁂ ⁂ ⁂

So now you know all about my first week in Tidwell Towers. It was sort of terrifying, sort of embarrassing, and sort of disgusting.

I'm guessing that my life here will never be "sort of average" again. And if more weird stuff happens to me, you'll be the first to know.

IF I LIVE TO TELL ABOUT IT, THAT IS.

THE END

OTIS DOODA

STRANGE BUT TRUE

BONUS MATERIALS

GOFISH

QUESTIONS FOR THE AUTHOR

ELLEN POTTER

© Shai Enav

What did you want to be when you grew up?

A writer. Big surprise, right? I've been writing stories ever since I could string words together. I always used to write about horses when I was a kid. The horse was always "glossy black" and owned by a series of villains until he finally wound up in the possession of a young girl who looked suspiciously like me. As you can see, I loved the book *Black Beauty*. As you can also see, there is a fine line between being inspired by someone else's book and out-and-out stealing from someone else's book.

When did you realize you wanted to be a writer?

This was really a big-deal moment for me: My school librarian knew how fast I devoured books, so she was always ready with a new book recommendation. One day, she told me I should read *Harriet the Spy* by Louise Fitzhugh. I found it on the bookshelf and started reading it right there, in the aisle. All of a sudden I *knew* the best books in the world were written for eleven-year-olds. That was great, because I was eleven. But I would be twelve in just a few short months. And after that, I'd be a teenager, and then I'd be an adult and I'd forget all about those great books I read when I was eleven. That was so tragic, I could hardly stand to think about it. So I vowed that since I couldn't always be an eleven-year-old reader, I would become a writer for eleven-year-olds. And that's what happened, more or less.

What's your most embarrassing childhood memory?
I have done so many klutzy, embarrassing things in my life that it's hard to remember them all. One of my most embarrassing moments, however, occurred when I was in college and studying abroad in England. Once a semester we had this big fancy dinner with the president of the college. It was a very hoity-toity sort of thing. During dinner, I was really pleased to see that the president was taking a great interest in me. He listened carefully when I spoke, watching me with an almost quizzical expression. *Maybe he finds my American accent charming,* I thought. But then the girl next to me whispered, "Pardon me, but there's something on your head." I reached up and from the top of my head I removed a piece of lettuce the size of an IHOP pancake.

What's your favorite childhood memory?
When I was home sick, my mother used to read *Mary Poppins* to me. I loved that.

What was your favorite thing about school?
I loved school, especially high school. I went to the High School of Music & Art, the school on which they based the movie *Fame*. Everyone was pretty quirky there, so cliques were virtually unheard of. It was a great school for all us oddball kids.

What was your least favorite thing about school?
Math. I literally could give myself a fever trying to sort out algebra.

What was your first job, and what was your "worst" job?

My first job was working at a Baskin-Robbins ice cream store. I worked there in the middle of winter in New York City. Most of our customers were police officers and thugs, and you know what? A bizarrely large percentage of both of them ordered rum-raisin ice cream. I have no idea what the significance of that is. I'm just saying.

My worst job was as a temporary receptionist at Ralph Lauren. My first assignment was to go to the grocery store and pick out twenty-six perfect lemons to display in a bowl in the waiting room. Have you ever found twenty-six perfect lemons? No? That's because there aren't any.

Where do you write your books?

I used to be very fussy about where I wrote. I only wrote in busy cafés with comfy seats and great medium-roast coffee. Then I had a baby. After that I wrote in public restrooms, underneath cars, in coat closets . . . any place really where I could get a few minutes of quiet.

Of the books you've written, which is your favorite?

I am always asked that question during school visits, and I always respond with my own question: "If you asked your parents which kid in the family was their favorite, what would they say?"

Most kids answer, "They'd say they love us all the same."

That's how I feel about my books. They all delight me and frustrate me for different reasons, but I love them all.

What challenges do you face in the writing process, and how do you overcome them?

I often worry I am not smart enough to be a writer. You may think that's very silly because I've already published so many books. Still, every time I sit down to write, I think, "Just who do you think you are, Ellen Potter? You . . . a writer? Ha!"

To overcome this, I tell myself that writing is not about how clever you are; it's about trying to understand your characters. It's about knowing why they are doing what they're doing and imagining how they must feel while they're doing it.

And if that fails to convince me, I pull out all the books I've written and say to myself, "Look, you ridiculous person, who do you think wrote all those books? YOU did. Now get to work!"

Which of your characters is most like you?

I considered telling you I was just like one of the Hardscrabbles in *The Kneebone Boy*, because they strike me as singularly brave and bold and smart. And since most of you don't know me personally, you'd never suspect I was lying. But just in case I *do* meet one of you someday, I feel I'd better come clean and say I'm not like them at all.

I suppose if I had to choose one character I am most like it would be Jeremy, the sister of the narrator in my book *Slob*. Like her, I also joined a club in elementary school comprised of girls who wanted to be boys. I don't know, I guess we all thought boys had it better than girls somehow. Anyway, we all cut our hair short and gave ourselves boy names (mine was indeed Jeremy). The club was short-lived because we wrote our boy names on our homework assignments, confusing our teacher to no end, and got into a heap of trouble for it.

What makes you laugh out loud?

Farts. I'm giggling right now, just writing the word. I used to suspect this made me very immature. Recently, though, I heard that Einstein also cracked up whenever someone farted, so I figure I'm in good company.

Who is your favorite fictional character?
There are many, but here are a few: the BFG from Roald Dahl's *The BFG*; Luna Lovegood from Harry Potter; Harriet M. Welsch from *Harriet the Spy*; Katniss Everdeen from *The Hunger Games*.

If you were stranded on a desert island, who would you want for company?
Someone who was more important than I am, so that people would send out search parties.

If you could travel in time, where would you go and what would you do?
I'd spend an evening with the Brontë girls and redo their hair.

What's the best advice you have ever received about writing?
Write every day.

I used to groan at this advice until I realized why it was so true. Think about this: When you have a friend whom you call every day, your conversations are usually effortless and flowing. But if you have a friend whom you only call once every few months, the conversation is often awkward until you get used to each other again. It's the same thing with writing. You want to visit your fictional worlds every day so that you can connect with them quickly and skip that awkward getting-to-know-you-again phase.

Do you ever get writer's block? What do you do to get back on track?
I get writer's block ALL the time. I used to worry it meant I wasn't a good writer. Now I know most writers deal with it on a regular basis. My go-to solution for writer's block is pretty simple: Take a walk. Walking helps me to think and I almost always come back home with a new idea.

What do you wish you could do better?
I'm lousy at almost everything except writing, so I'm afraid that would be a very long list.

What would you do if you ever stopped writing?
I'd own a candy store. And then I'd have all my teeth pulled out and have fake ones put back in so I wouldn't have to worry about cavities.

What do you want readers to remember about your books?
That they didn't want them to end.

SQUARE FISH

GO FISH

QUESTIONS FOR THE ILLUSTRATOR

DAVID HEATLEY

What did you want to be when you grew up?
An artist and a musician.

When did you realize you wanted to be an illustrator?
I wrote and illustrated my own homemade books since I was in preschool. My six-year-old version of "Peter and the Wolf" still survives and is my proudest work from that period.

What's your most embarrassing childhood memory?
I compulsively picked my nose and wiped it on my bedroom wall when I was eight. When friends came over, I would hang up a blanket to cover it, terrified that they would see behind it and realize I was a nose-picker.

What's your favorite childhood memory?
I've just gotten out of the bath and put on pajamas and the whole family snuggles on the couch together watching the original *Star Trek*. My mom falls asleep first.

SQUARE FISH

What was your first job, and what was your "worst" job?
My first jobs were babysitting and helping after school at a kindergarten. Worst job would have to be working at my college dining hall as "salad bar guy." I quit after two weeks.

Where do you work on your illustrations?
I have a studio about twenty blocks from my house on an industrial block of Woodside, Queens. I have a drafting table there, a long computer desk with a scanner and printer, a large flat file to keep my artwork, and even some musical instruments so I can record songs when I get ideas. I recorded all the songs for the first Otis Dooda soundtrack there. Have a listen! www.otisdooda.bandcamp.com

Where do you find inspiration for your illustrations?
Writing is always the most important part of any story, so I take my cues from the words themselves and see what pictures they create in my mind. The illustrations have to amplify the text, not the other way around. The way I draw is kind of a continuation of how I drew as a child. It took some time for me to strip away things I learned or copied from other artists that didn't belong to the way I draw. Now, my drawing style just feels natural. I don't really think about it at all.

Where do you go for peace and quiet?
I love hiking in the woods on mountains and near lakes. I also love the Mall / Literary Walk in Central Park. It's one of my favorite spots in the whole city. There are 100-year-old elm trees that form a canopy above you like a cathedral.

What makes you laugh out loud?
In-jokes with my oldest friends, who know me the best. Or my brothers when we reminisce about our crazy childhood together,

usually at the expense of my crazy dad. He used to bring lamb bones with him as a snack in the car when we went to the movies. He was totally asking for it!

Who is your favorite fictional character?

There's a flamboyant character named Zebra from the Sweet Pickles series that I had as a kid (and re-bought for my own kids). I absolutely love him. I'm also reading *Captain Easy* with my son and enjoying it immensely. It's an old Sunday newspaper comic strip from the 1930s.

What's the best advice you have ever received about illustrating?

Don't send your work all over to hundreds of places. Choose a few people that you really want to work for and send them special packages over a long period of time. That's how I got my work into the *New York Times* and on the cover of the *New Yorker.*

What do you want readers to remember about your books?

I want them to feel the love I poured into them. When I was a kid and I read a book where I could tell that the illustrator poured so much time and energy into something for ME, just a KID . . . it blew my mind. I felt really loved. I hope kids feel some of that same love when they look at my drawings.

What would you do if you ever stopped illustrating?

I do advertising and marketing work for money, but illustration usually has a part in everything I do. I think like a picture-maker and try to solve puzzles visually.

What do you consider to be your greatest accomplishment?

Marrying my wife, Rebecca, and being Maya and Sam's father. Hands down.

What would your readers be most surprised to learn about you?

I write goofy rap songs and sometimes like to break-dance.

What was your favorite thing about school?

English class and art class. I had great teachers who encouraged me to let my mind roam freely and discover what I loved. I was able to see a place for myself in the arts world because there were so many books and images out there that spoke to me.

If you could travel anywhere in the world, where would you go and what would you do?

I'd love to go to Japan and see some really early manga art, like Suihō Tagawa's *Norakuro* pages in person.

Who is your favorite artist?

It changes a lot. Jim Henson has been a pretty consistent source of inspiration since I was little.

What is your favorite medium to work in?

I like drawing by hand with pencils and pens, and then coloring on the computer. I'd love to do more hand-drawn animation with a full team of people the way it used to be done.

What was your favorite book or comic/graphic novel when you were a kid? What's your current favorite?
My favorite comic books were *X-Men* and *Spider-Man*. I was a Marvel guy. Now, I like more grown-up stuff like Chris Ware's comics.

What were your hobbies as a kid? What are your hobbies now, aside from illustrating?
I used to like to build robots and cities out of cardboard and play kickball. Now, I make things out of cardboard with my kids and play basketball.

What challenges do you face in the artistic process, and how do you overcome them?
The biggest challenge is when you're on a project and you feel like it's not very good or it's different from what you're used to doing. Some of my mentors taught me that you need to get used to that feeling. That if you feel a little scared and unsure of what you're creating, that's a sign that you're onto a new direction. Keep going! Also, be patient. Give yourself ten years to get good at something!

Get ready for more crazy Tidwell Towers adventures—OTIS DOODA is back!

Keep reading for a sneak peek!

THIS IS 100% NOT A LIE

One thing you should know about me is that I don't lie. Not very much, anyway. I don't have anything against lying. It's just that I'm bad at it. Whenever I tell a lie, I sweat like a pig in a bacon factory. Plus, I start talking like an eighty-year-old man.

The reason I'm telling you this is because you are probably going to think this book is made up. It's not. It's all 100% true. The thing is, some weird stuff has happened to me since I moved to New York City this past summer. You might have heard about some of it.

But now there's more.

If there's one thing I can't stand, it's the morning of the first day of school. You wake up all tired and wobbly because you've been staying up late the whole summer. Then you have to go to the bathroom and brush things that you haven't brushed for a while and get dressed before you've even watched any TV.

It's unnatural.

That morning, my older brother, Gunther, and I sat slumped at the

kitchen table, looking miserable while shoveling cereal into our mouths.

Mom was in a great mood, though.

"Aren't you guys excited?" she said. "A new school in *New York City*!"

"No," we both said at the same time.

But *she* sure was excited. You know why? Because she was finally going to get rid of us for a few hours. I know that's true because I saw it in her text message to Dad. Mom and Dad text-message when they want to tell each other things they don't want us to hear. Then later, when Mom goes to the bathroom, I look at her cell phone and see what's really going on.

Gunther looked at me over his cereal bowl with this cheesy smile on his face.

"You know what happens to new kids, don't you?" he said.

"What?" I said. I knew I shouldn't ask, but I couldn't help myself. I'd never actually been the new kid at a school before.

"The only person who'll sit next to you is the kid who digs in the treasure box," Gunther said.

"What does that mean?"

"Digging . . . in . . . the . . . treasure . . . box." Gunther demonstrated by pretending to pick his nose.

The funny thing is, I have never seen Gunther *actually* pick his nose. Since he's a pretty

disgusting guy in general, this always seemed strange to me. I once asked Mom about it.

"Maybe it's because he has good manners," she said.

But we both knew that was ridiculous. So she gave me a stern look and said, "Let's not talk about it, okay? It's very upsetting to Gunther."

That's why I like to bring it up every once in a while.

"Hey, that reminds me, Gunther," I said, "why don't you pick your nose? Are you afraid of the boogeyman?"

Gunther threw a Cheerio at me and hit me right in the eyeball. I flicked a spoon of milk at his head. Mom walked back in, took one look at us, and started text-messaging Dad like mad.

HANG ON A SECOND...

The fun's not over! Head over to:

to continue the madness! You'll find ACTIVITIES to do at home or school, OTIS' BEST BUILDERS BLOG, where you can show off your own brick creations and, best of all, a full-length original music SOUNDTRACK to the book you just read...

Plus more!